AVA WEST

Xander

Cover art by Shower of Schmidt Designs
Editing by Full Bloom Editorial

This book was professionally typeset on Reedsy.
Find out more at reedsy.com

To my husband,
Without you, this would not be possible. Without your support, love, and dedication to making my dream a reality, I would not be where I am today. I love you with my whole heart.

Contents

Chapter 1

Xander

Everything seemed so goddamn mediocre. I was supposed to be enthralled by all aspects of the MC life, but really, who could blame me for being bored? I'd been the head of this club for fifteen years, and every day it was the same thing.

Being President of the Black Stallions, I dealt with the business and recruiting. It was boring work, and I missed being a muscle. Don't get me wrong, I loved being the Prez. I loved leading my guys into better times than my dad ever did. Above all, I was a natural protector. I stood by my brothers through thick and thin, but more importantly to me, I protected the biker girls and old ladies.

All life experience shaped and influenced people. Mine told me that the women in the club took a lot of fucking shit, and they needed someone looking out for them. All clubs' rules differed, and the San Jose Black Stallions were no different. The way we were unique was that I had my Sacred Law. What was Sacred Law? No one, and I mean no one, was allowed to ever hurt my girls. That was the easiest way to get on my worst side.

My mom had been club property, and I would never desire the atrocities I saw happen to her on anyone, not even my worst goddamn enemy. I sure as hell didn't want any of the bitches that took care of me and my guys to be hurt the way my mom had been.

I generally spent my days in the public clubhouse, a simple biker bar at the edge of San Jose. It used to be that those discolored walls, abused, peeling linoleum floors, and busted up tables would bring me excitement and pump me up for whatever was coming next, but I just couldn't bring myself there. I hated to admit it, but the slump started about the time Annie dumped my ass for her side piece a year ago.

"Annie" or Keyanna Sinclair and I had a nice thing for a bit. Sex was great. She was sweet, funny, charismatic, and very understanding. What was there not to like? Annie wasn't a Black Stallions girl, just a normal woman I met in a bar that liked me. She didn't know anything about me, my chapter, or my lifestyle which made things simple. She knew I was a biker but didn't know if I was a weekend warrior or what. Then, one day, while pumped from some club shit that went down, I spilled to her. She had done her research by this time and knew exactly who I was, what I did, but we didn't talk about it. She didn't seem upset or bothered by the things I told her other than it involved people she knew. Her best friend, indirectly.

We didn't mention it again until the day she broke up with me. She said she couldn't handle the crimes on my hands, worrying it would come back on her— but I knew better. It had nothing to do with me. Annie had never been scared of me before, but she was then. She was sweating and her pupils dilated with intense terror. She was breaking things off with me because her high school sweetheart had come back to town for her best friend's wedding, and she acted like I was going to kill her. Sure, that was generally how things in our circumstance would've gone down, given the things she knew, but I wasn't stupid. I wasn't going to do that in front of other people. She would be "dealt with" and then the cleaners would come in. It would be like she skipped town, and no one would bat an eye at it.

That wasn't how things ended up though. Annie made sure of that after I

2

shot her honey. She said she had recorded everything I ever told her. In the event of her or her dude's death, someone forwarded everything to the cops— so I was stuck, sitting on my fucking hands.

A lot of my crew broke off after that. They thought I had lost my nerve, that I was going soft, but I wasn't going to risk our club over some scorned lover bullshit. Keyanna Sinclair and Zane Taylor could have their happily ever after, but they would both be disposed of if she talked.

Annie was thirty when we dated. Since her, I made a rule not to get involved with a woman younger than forty.

I tried convincing my little brother, Austin, to join up so day-to-day would be a bit more entertaining, but he refused. He was too busy with a band as head of security. I couldn't blame him. He made a great living and Bruce Mayes was a great guy. Hook was his club name, but he pretty much just partied with us. His wife, Sally, was amazing. Don't get me started on their adorable kids, Jesse and Jessa. Sure, they were just babies, but they had their father's talent for commanding a room with a toothy smile and adorable laugh.

Now, stranded with my gang, every day blended together. Not all of it was bad. I got my choice of the Black Stallions girls to take to bed every night, but there was only so much time they could preoccupy. After doing the same shit for so long, things became boring and mundane.

My club, sex, drugs, none of it interested me.

As I took a swig from my beer bottle and slammed the bottle onto the table, a wooden shard broke off the side— like almost every time I did that. I needed to stop, or I would need to buy a new one. I hadn't done that in ten years. I caught the distinct sound of the creaky, rusted out hinges of the door. I turned and saw my old friend, Bruce, walk in. Usually, I had to go to check up on him. He rarely came to the clubhouse. Even more surprising was the smoking hot babe that strolled in behind.

She had long, dark chocolate hair that bounced around her shoulders, like dark water rolling against sand. Sun-kissed skin of a biker looked so natural with her olive undertones. Light freckling spilled across her face and trickled down her cleavage. Those bright blue eyes reminded me of the crystal-clear ocean hitting the surf.

She couldn't have been older than twenty-five. Tits nearly bursting out of her tight tank top and her plump ass was form-fit to that tight leather skirt. Her toned legs were on full display thanks to the short hemmed skirt and her black high heel boots. She wore a weathered denim jacket that was big on her— a man's jacket. Fuck, she was a damn vision, like a young Megan Fox.

Fuck, she was hot with an "I don't give a fuck" attitude. It was drawing me in. Too bad I had sworn off girls that young. I was forty-five. I needed a woman with experience in the bedroom and life. It didn't mean I wasn't enjoying the show, though.

She jumped a bit as Domino strolled in behind her, the door creaking angrily. The melody of loud engines outside rolled like thunder through the air. She was squinting from the thick smoke in the air and the dimmed, weak lights. Her phone dropped out of her hand and clattered with the dusty linoleum. She spun around, giving me a full view of the back of her jacket. Her ass was magnificent, but it was the patch that caught my attention.

Black Stallions
Sydney, AS
Est. 1981

She was a fuckin ol' lady? Unlikely. I had been studying her from the moment she sauntered through the door, and she didn't carry herself like a kept woman.

She strutted like a model without the whole conceitedness. She knew she was drop dead gorgeous but didn't overly flaunt it. She probably didn't pick that outfit to make every man in the room stare, but that was inevitable. Even if she were wearing a potato sack, I doubt any fewer eyes would be watching her.

All eyes were on her once everyone caught a glimpse. I was intrigued, salivating, and eager to find out who she was, and what she was doing in my clubhouse.

She righted herself and her eyes moved to Bruce quizzically before he said something to her.

"Hey, Bruce!" I called at him. He turned, a big grin on his face. With a gritty hand on the small of her leather skirt, he guided her through the crowd toward me.

I was a bit curious about this "woman." I couldn't help wondering why the hell she showed up at my public clubhouse.

There was only one reason anyone brought a female into the clubhouse. It was one of the simple needs of the male species— to bang. Women drifted to us bikers, to pledge themselves to the Black Stallions as our whores and do whatever we wanted to. I doubted that was why Bruce led this girl through our rickety door.

I couldn't deny a man could fuck other women behind his wife's back, but Bruce wasn't like that. He had been all about Sally since he met her, and he was not looking at this girl with anything other than protection and concern. Women always threw themselves at him, even though he'd got hitched. Bruce had more pussy at his feet than Johnny Wadd ever did.

But what made me even more curious, was that the female didn't look at him

5

with any type of interest, more like he was a means to an end, someone doing her a favor.

Who are you, sexy bitch?

"Hey, brother." I hugged Bruce and noticed the girl perched on a bar stool by him, back straight with confidence. She didn't seem worried about where she was. Strange.

This girl did not look scared at all. You would think she was sitting in a restaurant instead of a clubhouse. She had the commanding presence of a Dominatrix and the allure of a siren to sailors. She was something special. That was for sure.

"Hey, who's the broad?" I probed, and he glanced at her over his shoulder. We walked a few feet away as she sat there, taking in her surroundings. Her body relaxed the more she looked around at my rough crowd and took in the stank emitted in the air. It was a mixture of booze, smoke, and sweat. I had gotten used to it a long time ago. Maybe she hadn't been around it before, but she didn't seem bothered by it.

"She's one of my band mate's cousins. You know Liam. She moved in with him a few days ago from Australia." I slowly nodded. Sounded simple enough, but it left me with more questions than he answered.

"What is she doing here? You know the rule about girls who enter the clubhouse, man." I cocked an eyebrow at him, and he chuckled. My rules were pretty simple. Don't bring a bitch to the clubhouse unless she was Black Stallion's property. Only club property, den mothers, and house mouses were allowed past the threshold. End of story.

"She's a Bred In, Gunner." That was surprising. Why had I never seen her before? I was sure I wouldn't forget a beauty like her. Bred In was the term for the daughter of a member. It was a title to state that they were untouchable. How could she be a Bred In if she moved here recently? Was her Pops from the area? Did she come here from living with her mother or college or whatever she was doing? The original Black Stallions had their chapter in Australia. Was that where she was a Bred In? Well, it explained how comfortable she was in the clubhouse.

"A Bred In? From whom?" I asked immediately.

"She's a big girl. She can handle herself with bikers. She may look sweet, but that girl can be scary. Her name is Jen Saunders. Her dad was the founding father." I didn't know whether to be frightened or impressed.

"Trapper is her dad?" Bruce slowly nodded.

Trapper was a fucking legend in the biker community. If you didn't know who he was, you learned fast. I met him once, years ago. We had a meeting when my chapter split off from his. It was amicable, but that man even scared me. Trapper was psychotic. I wasn't under the disillusion that bikers like me and Trapper weren't insane to an extent, but Trapper took it to a new level. He told me a drunken story about chopping off the dick of any asshole he heard about screwing his daughter. Was this the same daughter he was talking about?

"Was. Officers killed him three weeks ago, and she ran here to Liam. He named her his heiress, and some of his officers weren't happy at being run by a woman." Wow. How did I not hear about this until now? It was usually big news when one of the top five in a chapter died. That kind of news spread like wildfire even this far away.

Naming a female as the next president of a chapter was one of the best ways to insight a war between chapters. A female president was enough to break down even the most vicious clubs. That was the deal in an outlaw club.

Women were at the very bottom of the chain as far as bikers were concerned. Even if she was patched, which was doubtful. It did happen, but it was rare, and the woman had to be a hard-ass like the men. She had to be able to roll with the punches.

"Holy shit, man. Trapper is gone?" Hook frowned intensely.

"Her uncle stole her position and tried to force her into being property. She ran. End of story."

Well, fuck. That was one line my men didn't fucking cross. Whores were whores by choice. If it's by force, it's rape and that did not fly. I held my men to higher standards. Some presidents didn't care, and tried to start wars with me over it, but I didn't budge. Jen was sexy, but that didn't mean I would let any of my guys fuck her against her will.

It used to be like that under my dad's rule. He didn't care which is why my woman during those years, Laura, was kept away from every other man in the club. No one was allowed near her, and it was that way until I met Annie.

I didn't mind my guys having a good time with the girls, but rape was a no-go. The girls knew this was their life. Rarely did any of the girls put up a fight. If they did, my men knew to take a step back and I would come in and set her straight. The bitches knew what our expectations of them were, and they did their duty, or they would be given to someone who wouldn't be nearly as nice as me and my guys.

"Again, why is she here?" He turned nervous.

"I need a favor." That was what it always came down to with everyone. They needed help. His expression morphed sheepishly as he kicked his shoe against the dust on the floor.

CHAPTER 1

"What kind?" My head snapped at the sound of a glass breaking against the counter. The bartender gave me an indifferent look as he cleaned it up. Damn amateur.

"I know you're still looking for a bartender for the other bar your guys frequent. She's a bartender and fucking amazing at her job, brother. She made some drinks for the band last night that were top-notch." I had a hard time believing that his experience had anything to do with my guys' needs. We didn't do those top-notch bomb drinks with swirly straws. We were rather simple, beers and straight liqueur. Plus, the girl would need to be cool with the drugs my guys brought to the table.

"You want me to give a job to a chick I don't know?" I was about to laugh in his face from that. I only gave jobs to people I knew wouldn't fuck up. Just because Trapper was her Pops didn't mean squat to me. I didn't know this girl, and I had never had a drink she prepped so the answer was a definite no unless she could impress me in one way or another.

Then I saw something incredible. Drill, one of my newer patched members, strolled right over to her with confidence and sex dripping from his eyes. He blocked her against the bar and her sky-blue eyes lifted to him. I didn't hear what he said, but she roughly grabbed his head and forced it hard against her knee. I could hear the crack of either his bones or his teeth from a few feet away.

My jaw dropped as I watched him shield his face. That sexy bitch hit like a fucking man.

Next, she stood up, gripped his shoulder and lodged her knee into his stomach. Last, she kicked him straight in the balls, and poor Drill crumbled to the floor, cupping his nuts. The room went stone-cold silent. Some of my guys looked at her with fear, some were gawking with amusement. I was staring at her in fucking lust.

"Don't ever call me 'doll'," she threatened in a voice sweet as honey. She had an accent, a thick, delicious accent that made my dick throb.

If I were to name two things in this world that were my biggest turn-ons, it would be a woman who could kick some serious ass and a woman with an accent. In my book, she couldn't possibly be more attractive than she was at that moment, standing over Drill.

I could feel the blood stopped at my pole, making it impossible to think of anything else. Screw my promise to myself. I hadn't been this excited about a woman in a long time. That was unsettling. The last time I got anywhere near this excited was Annie, and we know how that turned out. It was apparent that she was nothing like Annie, though. Jen was a tough babe.

This girl was hot enough to be a Sports Illustrated model, and what was I? A forty-five-year-old chapter president that looked like a fucking muscle. I wasn't ugly, but I was no Bruce Mayes either. Women flocked to me because of my position and tattoos, girls mainly into mature men and bikes, or they heard my dick was pierced and were curious about it.

I doubt I had much of a chance. I was old enough to be her dad. Who knows? Maybe she was into the whole Daddy thing. Doubted it, though.

"I'm going for a smoke, Bruce." She glanced over at my good friend, who nodded. Her eyes drifted to me. A flirtatious smirk rose across my lips, and she stared at me as she slipped off her jacket. I waited to see her reaction, but she didn't show one. She turned and made a runway walk out of the clubhouse, thrusting her middle finger in the air. A bunch of cheering from the bitches sounded through the room. I chuckled proudly as the rusty door squeaked to a halt, slamming against the steel frame. It was a closed curtain to the scene she just presented to the entire club.

"Okay, she's hired."

Bruce raised a brow at me, surprised. Yup, Jen had even affected me, and I think he knew it. "Really?"

I slowly nodded, smirking in the direction she disappeared in. "Any girl who can flatten one of my guys is gold in my book." Damn straight.

Chapter 2

Jen

Some men were such pigs. That doofus had the gall to call me 'doll' of all things! He deserved the kick in the balls. I may hail from a near-desert, but I was more of a cobra than a flower. That was one good thing I got from my dad, my thick skin.

It's been both a blessing and a curse. Guys I've dated said I was an unfeeling demon. When things ended, I'd shrug it off and move on. I didn't really know what love was. It was a casualty of growing up in the club. When your father is a biker legend like Donald Saunders, you learn to trust no one. That's one reason why I would never let myself get dragged down by a biker. I saw what my dad's lifestyle did to my mom.

He screwed around on her constantly, and she cried herself to sleep every single night while he was out with the guys. He had his whores, and that was what killed my mom. It wasn't the drugs or the criminal activity that did her in, it was the way my dad treated her like she wasn't the best thing that ever happened to him. He should've seen her as that. She loved him with her whole heart, and he crushed her every single day.

If there was ever a person in this world that I loved, it was my mom, and she was why I refused to ever let myself get sucked in by a biker that way. I had never even slept with a biker, and I planned to keep it that way. The guys in my chapter knew not to fuck with me in any way, shape, or form.

The only thing tempting to change my mind was the biker that Bruce had been talking to. Bruce wasn't a biker, but he was a part of the chapter. That was confusing as hell. I didn't get how someone could be one and not the other.

The man that talked to Bruce had caught my attention. He was a bit rough, scarred across his jaw and through one of his eyebrows. Quite the silver fox. He had thick salt and pepper hair, a trimmed beard, and honey-hazel eyes. He had light crow's feet around his eyes, but he didn't have wrinkles other than that.

A white t-shirt, a Black Stallion's leather vest, and dark jeans covered his muscular, tattooed body. I doubted even a leather jacket could hide those bulges.

What was wrong with me? Why the hell would I check him out? I would never get involved with someone like him. Bikers were man-whores. Who knows what diseases I could catch from him! Ugh!

I had to admit. He was ruggedly attractive and there was... something there. Like an undeniable connection between two people who didn't know a single thing about each other. It was something I had only ever read about in ridiculous romance novels. Two strangers locking eyes and feeling an intensity, a connection, a desire form. They would find each other, talk, realize they were soulmates destined to get married, have kids, and live happily ever after.

I scoffed at the thought. As if! I wasn't an idiot. That man had every biker bitch at his disposal to satisfy every desire he had. That wasn't me.

I was nowhere close to being a virgin, but I wasn't a slut either. Just because a biker asked me to suck his dick didn't mean I would. Even if it was that attractive silver fox.

I rubbed my hand up the back of my shirt under the fabric, feeling the still sore bruises of my uncle's force. I knew my dad was an idiot. He actually thought he could get away with naming me as his heiress. Like I could ever be the president of the Sydney Black Stallions chapter. No one was going to stand for it, and Dad paid for that with his life. My punishment for his stupid decision was my Uncle Ronny, Crack, trying to force me into being a whore to his buddies. Like he thought I had forced my dad to name me his heiress. He accused me of sleeping with my father to manipulate him. Ew!

My dad had foreseen someone trying to force themselves on me at one point in my life, and he gave me the necessary skills to escape the situation. No man that came at me that night left unscathed— Crack included.

I escaped the clubhouse and ran to my cousin from my mom's side of the family, Liam. I spent a couple of days at his place before I finally told him what happened, why I was running from Crack, and why I could never go back to Sydney.

I knew Crack had a hit on me now. Luckily, I did have allies in his organization who were loyal to me. Mostly, the newer guys, ol ladies, and bitches.

When Liam suggested going to the local clubhouse, I almost bolted. I knew what would happen if my uncle found me. I would be killed and buried with my dad if I was lucky. It was the only way for Crack to ensure that I didn't take away his power. I didn't want it, but he didn't give me a chance to tell him that. He just jumped on the, "let's turn my niece into a whore against her will" train.

14

Liam told me the local chapter disassociated with the Sydney Black Stallions because of 'Gunner'. He was the president of the chapter and didn't go by the same rules as the other presidents. He did right by his men, but didn't allow certain things that other clubs shrugged at. If Gunner agreed that I was right in running, Liam said he wouldn't turn me in to Crack. I was willing to take the chance of getting protection from my psychotic uncle if Gunner was really how Liam described.

Liam contacted Bruce, who took me to the public clubhouse. It looked like all the other clubhouses I had ever been to. The intention was to introduce me to Gunner, but unless he was the jackass I kicked in the balls, it didn't happen. I wasn't surprised that the doofus biker had the balls to ask me to drop to my knees and suck him off. Normally, I would've laughed at him and told him that he wasn't man enough to handle me, but then he added 'doll'.

No one called me a doll. I would go Biker Lola Bunny on their asses for even uttering a syllable of that disgusting word.

The bikers used to call me that when I was a kid, and it always pissed me off. If someone wanted to see the biker in my DNA, call me a fucking doll.

Strolling out the front door of the biker bar, I took notice of the parking lot. I hadn't been paying attention before. I noticed the bikes, of course, but one thing I noticed then was the distressed and peeling paint on the cement walls outside the bar. It looked like once there had been a mural of a woman with light blonde hair and purple eyes, but the paint was so aged, I could barely tell it had ever been there. She was pretty, though.

The mural had a caption. *RIP Davina Devereaux.* Was she one of the girls from the chapter? Why was there a mural of her? Her picture left so many questions.

I pulled out a cigarette and lit it up as I kicked one of the many pieces of gravel in the parking lot.

Scuffs and scratches covered some bikers, while a select few shined like a new penny. There were two pickup trucks, one being Bruce's, and a four-door painted cherry red. That car was probably the bartenders' vehicle. He didn't seem like a truck kind of guy. I was curious who the big, mist blue Silverado with a massive Harley in the bed belonged to.

That bike was beautiful. It had the black diamond with red outlining near the front tire which I smirked at. Kudos to the One Percenter.

"That one is Gunner's," Bruce stated as he walked out of the bar and I stood up, tossing down my smoke.

"Hmm. It's nice." It was true. The bike was in perfect condition. It made me miss my bike.

I strolled over to Bruce's truck and climbed in. His truck was pretty old and beaten up for a rockstar. I was surprised and not at the same time. Everyone had heard of his band, Mayes, and I fangirled when I got to meet his wonderful wife, Sally. I wasn't a Mayes fan until she joined his team. Sally Mayes was my Justin Bieber.

"Did you talk to Gunner?" I inquired to Bruce, as he drove me out of the parking lot, and he nodded.

"Yeah, all is good. He was pretty impressed by you." I looked at him perplexed. What had I done that could impress someone?

"Impressed?"

He nodded and smirked. "When you dropped Drill, the biker who approached you. Gunner respects any woman who can go toe-to-toe with him or any of his guys."

That was surprising. Most guys hated strong women like me, so scrutiny wasn't surprising.

"Really?"

He grinned. "Yeah. I got you a job at a bar they run. They need a bartender, and he liked you. That's a big deal, just so you know. Gunner doesn't like many people. He tolerates most people." Sounds like something we have in common.

"Ripper." I didn't have much else to say without sounding like a bitch. I didn't want to seem ungrateful to Bruce. He was nice, for a guy. I was a bit untrusting of guys. I guess that came with my uncle trying to get me gang raped.

"A bit of friendly advice, Jen. Don't get involved with any of the bikers," he stated out of nowhere, and I gave him a sideways glance.

"I'm not into bikers. Trust me. It's not going to happen," I explained, and he nodded.

"Gunner is the only one of those guys that are even a bit trustworthy. He can get pretty possessive though."

"Why do you keep talking about him?" I sneered. It was a bit annoying. I wanted a silent car ride. I didn't even want to go to the clubhouse. It was Bruce's idea to take me to see Gunner. I was a bit uncomfortable being there considering what happened the last time I went to a clubhouse to meet bikers.

"I saw you guys looking at each other. I'm not blind," he explained, and I groaned.

"Who?"

"Gunner."

"I don't even know who he was in there." I was beyond agitated at this point. Why was Bruce doing this now?

"I was talking to him when you dropped Drill."

Oh. My. God. No. Not the silver fox.

"You mean the guy with the scar on his eyebrow?" I didn't want Bruce to know I paid much attention to him or that I had an attraction to him. Damn. I hoped to avoid the silver fox. He just became twice as off-limits as before. He was my new boss.

"Yup, that's Gunner."

I slowly nodded before looking out the window. I just wanted to climb back in bed and forget that man for now. Maybe I would remember him later when I was touching myself. In the shower. Relieving some tension. No, bad idea, Jen. I can't be giving in to these desires. It would make it seem too logical. It wasn't possible to even just fuck him. Maybe if he wasn't the president of the chapter, I could just fuck him and forget him. If he was just some random guy in a bar, I could fuck him then leave. I could get him out of my system, but that wasn't possible.

I would not become a whore for bikers. Not even for Gunner.

"His name is Xander. Xander Davenport." That was all Bruce said on the subject, and he dropped it. The rest of the ride was silent.

That name was repeating over and over in my head. Xander Davenport.

Xander. God, why was that name so fucking sexy and making my skin buzz with arousal?

Shit. This was going to be way harder than I thought. I was in trouble.

Okay. The first step was to admit I had a problem. I wanted Xander 'Gunner' Davenport. I wanted him bad, but I had to resist my lady bits trying to lead me to do something stupid.

Maybe I was just like my mom, and I was drawn in by something I thought I saw in him that wasn't there. If that were the case, I knew I was in trouble.

* * *

Hailee Steinfeld's *Flashlight* was blaring through my phone in my room at Liam's house, while I surfed the internet on my laptop. I was looking to see if I had any better job opportunities than working in a biker bar. Sadly, the other options were worse. Two strip clubs, three lesbian bars, and one bachelor party, and that was for one night. I put in an application for the bachelor party. At least that would bring in some extra cash, so I could get my own place.

I was frustrated and consigned to working in that biker bar. That didn't mean I had to be happy about it. If I worked there, Xander Davenport's temptation would be constant, and I wanted to stay away from that.

I slammed my computer shut and turned off the music before going downstairs.

Liam was the proud owner of a two-story, five bedroom house. The exterior was plastered in stucco and painted white with black shingles and matching shutters on the windows. There was a pool in the backyard and a pool house. The interior oozed chill— white walls, a few photographs hanging, and black leather furniture.

The living room had a ceiling high fireplace, two sofas, a glass coffee table, and soft, white carpet. It was the same carpet everywhere except the dining room and the kitchen.

Liam was cooking eggs in the modern kitchen that any housewife would kill for. His bodyguard, Trip, sitting at the mahogany kitchen table, playing on his phone like a teenager.

"Hey, Jen!" Liam smiled at me, and I returned it. We weren't close, but we used to be pen pals. He always said if I ever wanted to escape, his door was always open, and he lived true to his word. I would always be grateful to him for that.

"Liam, hey," I said, as I ran my fingers through my hair.

"How did it go at the bar?" he asked, while turning down the stove. Liam and Trip were gone when I arrived, so I hadn't gotten to tell Liam that I got offered a job by Xander.

"As could be expected, I guess." I strolled over to the fridge and grabbed a bottle of water from the drawer.

"Which means what exactly?" he asked and Trip snickered.

"She kicked one of my brother's asses." Trip grinned big, and Liam's jaw dropped.

"What?" He looked at me accusingly.

"He called me 'doll' and asked for a blow job. Well, asked would be putting it lightly. He demanded I drop to my knees. He was asking for an ass-whooping," I justified my actions and Trip laughed.

"Seriously? That's what he said to you?" I nodded, and Trip grinned big. "Way to go putting him in his place like that. He's new and doesn't know how things work yet. If the boss caught him saying that to you, I doubt he will be around much longer," Trip explained, and I was baffled. What was that supposed to mean? He was talking about Gunner, Xander, right?

"Why?" I asked as I took a seat across from Trip at the table.

"Because the boss has a thing for you. Obviously." My eyes widened. "I got a text from Hook. He said he saw it. Xander has telltale signs for those that know him. It's easy to tell once you get to know him. People that don't know him can't tell," Trip uttered, and I looked over to Liam who had his protective cousin mask on.

"Be careful there, Jen," Liam warned, and I rolled my eyes. I had already resigned myself. I was not going to fuck Xander Davenport no matter how much my pussy was begging for it.

"I don't date or fuck bikers. I'm going out to the pool." I waved to them, as I went out the back door.

I loved Liam's pool. He had a gate installed around the pool, loungers set up around the rectangular-shaped pool, and the pool house built a few feet from the pool. The pool house was more like a tiny house painted an ocean blue with yellow trim. The inside was like an island getaway with a hammock in the living room instead of couches. The small kitchen only had a microwave and a sink, no table or chairs. The bedroom in the back was simple. A queen sized bed with a bedside table and that was the extent of the pool house.

I went to the pool house and changed into my black string bikini. I stole some sunscreen and put on a good amount before walking out to the poolside. I put in my earbuds and turned on the music on my phone. Korn's *Coming Undone* filled my ears, and I relaxed against the lounger.

People thought I listened to a strange mix of music. I liked all kinds of music, but I listened to a lot of rock around the bikers back home. Korn and Incubus reminded me of my dad, and I was starting to miss him a lot.

If he had heard what Trip was saying about Xander, he would've done some pretty gnarly things to Xander for even looking at me. Most of the guys in the clubhouse would've lost their dicks. My dad was pretty protective of me, which was probably why Crack went so above and beyond with his punishment.

I was always Daddy's little girl in his eyes. Another reason why guys didn't stick around long. I didn't mind. That was for the best. I didn't want guys to stay around longer than they were useful. No use in leaving a string of broken hearts behind in my wake.

I must've dozed off because when I opened my eyes there were at least fifty people around. I sat up, pushing my sunglasses up my forehead.

Half were women, supermodel gorgeous with revealing bathing suits, and the other half were men wearing either swimming trunks or shorts that they were pretending were for swimming. It was a pool party. I think Liam mentioned it last night. It must've slipped my mind. I recognized a couple of the men from the clubhouse, and then I caught sight of him.

Xander Davenport. He looked so tasty. He was shirtless, showcasing his gorgeous tattoos and thick muscles, and he had on some black and gray swim trunks.

People were playing pool volleyball, and the ball hit right next to Xander. He picked it up and pegged it at one of his men, laughing happily. He might've been rough around the edges, but I was sure of one thing about him. When he laughed and smiled, he was beautiful. His teeth shined, and his eyes twinkled with enjoyment, accenting his crows feet around his eyes.

Then, his eyes met mine, and I knew he caught me— damn it.

Chapter 3

Xander

I was able to drag the information out of Bruce about the party Liam was hosting at his house. I knew this was a chance to get close to Jen again without seeming like a stalker. I wasn't looking to fuck her. At least, not yet. I could wait for that. I was a patient man.

Maybe I was breaking my rules, but I was never much for following rules. I had seen enough at the bar to know that I wanted her. Even if just in my bed. I knew not to expect a lot out of young women like her. I wasn't expecting a relationship or anything. I was a logical man. I was burned enough by Annie. I didn't need more pain.

I was bored, and Jen offered some entertainment. At least, that was what I was telling myself. I swore, sometimes I wasn't even sure of my intentions.

The only woman I had been with that hadn't burned me was Laura but I had burned her plenty. I knew that which was one thing that saddened me whenever I saw her. I saw the look on her face when she would see me. It was the whole "you hurt me and don't know how badly" look. She deserved better than me or the entire damn club.

Laura had been dragged into the club by my dad and tossed at me. From then on, she was my woman. Still, most guys wouldn't go near her just in case something was still going on between us. If it wasn't for my conquest of Jen, I probably would ask that woman back. I didn't think she would say yes though.

I went to the party and hung out with my men by the pool when I saw Jen staring at me.

I had seen her when I arrived. She looked gorgeous in that black bikini. I wasn't sure if she was just ignoring everyone or relaxing, but I figured the latter. The bathing suit looked so sexy on her, barely covering those delicious tits of hers. She was practically naked in that thing. Well, her tits were anyway. It was a black string bikini.

I decided to blend in with everyone until she made the first move, and she had. That one look.

I gave her my smirk that usually had women dropping their panties and winked at her. I wasn't sure if it was my effect on her or the sun, but her cheeks got an adorable shade of pink.

"Xan," Bruce got my attention and sat down next to me.

"Hey, brother." He gave me a knowing look.

"You know, you seem a bit like a stalker sitting here." I huffed and rolled my eyes.

"Man, she was staring at me, not the other way around."

"Sure, keep telling yourself that."

"Seriously." I drove it home, and he slowly nodded.

"Still. You're sitting over here while she is over there. What's up with that? You're not exactly the kind of guy that doesn't go in for the kill." I laughed at his joke.

"I'm taking my time with this." I looked over at Jen, and she had stopped staring at me. She was starting to sit up, as Sally walked over to her. Sally tried to hand her some disgusting pink drink, but Jen set it down. Hmm. Did she not drink?

"There is a difference between taking your time and wasting it. You're wasting it because you haven't even talked to her. Once you have talked to her, then it's taking your time." I chuckled and smirked at him.

"Yup, sure." He gave me a friendly slap on the shoulder.

"Word of the wise, Zane and Key are coming today. Don't cause too much trouble." Great. That was the last thing I wanted to deal with.

"Just peachy."

"Be nice, Xan," Bruce offered his advice, but it was futile.

"I am usually. It's Annie that causes a scene. You'd think a year would be long enough for her to get over me shooting him." Bruce laughed as I hopped to my feet. "Have some fun, brother." He nodded, as I walked around the pool. Sally was starting to stand up as I got over to them. "Hey, Sally." She turned and grinned at me. Her copper curls rolled over her shoulders and her blue eyes shimmered in the sunlight.

"Xander, hey!" She hugged me and I returned it, stealing a glance at Jen. The girl looked at me then looked away like she didn't think she was allowed to look at me. Did I make her nervous? I could tell by how her fingers shook that I affected her, but I wasn't sure if it was fear or desire filling her for me.

It was always one or the other, but it was a mixture of both in most cases.

"You look great, Sally," I said as I pulled back, and she grinned.

"Thanks. The baby weight is slowly coming off." I could tell she was slimming back up. She turned back to Jen who looked between the both of us with an unreadable expression. "Jen, you haven't touched your drink." Jen waved it off.

"No offense, Sal, but if it's not a normal alcohol color, I don't drink it. That's not a real drink." Interesting. She doesn't like girly drinks. I liked Jen a bit more already.

"What would you like?" Sally didn't seem offended which was normal for her. She didn't get upset much.

"Considering my cousin's selection, some Jack would be great." I didn't peg her for a whiskey drinker.

"Jack Daniels?" Sally asked, in surprise and Jen laughed.

"Casualty of growing up around bikers. I like the hard shit," she explained, and Sally shrugged.

"Do you want something, Xan?" I grinned at Sally. She was such a hostess even when she was at someone else's party.

"Just a beer. Thanks." She nodded and walked away. Sally had a look on her face that said she knew I was there to talk to Jen, and she seemed to approve. I hate to say it, but Sally's opinion didn't mean much. After all, she was happy for me and Annie, and look at how well that went. Straight down the toilet.

I took a seat on the lounger next to Jen and smirked at her.

"You gave Drill quite a beating, but I think you did the most of the damage to his ego." Her eyes met mine with wonder before she huffed.

"I assume he's never had his ass handed to him by a woman?" I shrugged a bit.

"Not since I've known him. You do that a lot?" I asked, and she rolled her eyes.

"I didn't have to until recently."

"Why's that?" Then she frowned. What did I say?

"My dad pretty much kept the assholes at bay." Oh. She was sad because of her dad dying. Fuck, I didn't want to upset her.

"Yeah, I heard about what happened. Sorry. He's pretty much a legend, even this far away. I met him one time a few years back," I said, and she slowly nodded.

"Yeah, I know. Story of my life." She slipped her sunglasses off her head and set them on the table.

"Yeah, my old man was like that, too," I said, and she looked at me curiously. "I took over when my dad passed away. Growing up, you either get away with shit or get severely punished just because of who your dad is." I explained, and she just stared at me for a minute.

"Yeah, something like that. My dad was a pretty scary guy to most people. Not surprising considering some shit I witnessed him do and get away with." There was a teasing tone to her voice and not a hint of fear. She was making a joke but wasn't kidding at all. I knew exactly what she meant. I witnessed a lot of crazy shit growing up myself.

"Yeah, what else is new?" she snickered, as Sally walked back over with the drinks.

"Xan, are you playing nice?" Sally handed me my beer and Jen the whiskey. Jen sat up and took a decent sip of her drink. She didn't shudder or anything from the burn of the alcohol.

"I always play nice." Sally rolled her eyes.

"Yeah, right. Jen, has he been a good boy?" Then, Jen laughed loud, nearly dropping her glass.

"You did not just ask me that." Jen kept laughing and Sally rolled her eyes. "I plead the fifth." I chuckled from her answer.

"Sally, leave these two alone." Bruce came up behind her and threw his arms around her.

"I'm not doing anything," Sally deflected.

"Hey, Jen." She raised her glass in Bruce's direction as a response. "Stay out of trouble, kid," Bruce said, and I noticed Jen's eyes darkened.

"Don't call me 'kid,'" she warned before setting down her drink. Bruce and Sally just stared at her. "I'm a twenty-seven-year-old woman. I've lived and seen ten times worse than anything you could comprehend. I'm giving you a free pass on the 'kid' this time," she said, then Bruce and Sally were distracted by some new arrivals, but my eyes were on Jen. A statement like that would've scared off a lot of people, but oddly enough, it turned me on. Fuck, I wanted her.

She didn't want people acting like she was a child. She had probably been treated like she couldn't do anything for herself most of her life. I knew it had been that way for me and Austin until my dad passed away. Once I became the president, everything changed, and I could get an identity for myself.

Shit. I never had understood someone else like this. That epiphany left me with a strange feeling in my chest. What the hell was it? I couldn't comprehend it. It was a tightening pressure mixed with a tingly sensation spreading out through my whole body. I had never felt anything like it before.

"Jen, this is Keyanna and Zane," Sally said, and I lifted my eyes to see my ex-girlfriend, her stomach round with a baby, and her husband standing by Sally. Yup, I was not looking forward to this.

"Hi," Jen muttered, sending a small wave, but Annie wasn't looking at her. She was scowling at me.

"Xander," she sneered at me, and I could feel Jen's eyes on me. I didn't look to see why she was staring.

"Hey, Keyanna." She stopped letting me call her Annie when we broke up. She considered it a pet name, and she hated it after I shot Zane. I turned my eyes to her husband who had a bit less animosity toward me than Annie did. "Zane," I greeted him monotoned, and he nodded. He always seemed indifferent about me, like I didn't matter to him even though I nearly killed him.

"Don't you have something better to be doing than hanging around here?" Annie scowled at me, and I rolled my eyes. I wasn't going to respond to that. I didn't need the aggravation, and I didn't want Jen thinking I was the kind of asshole that would get in an altercation with a pregnant woman. I may have been a crazy asshole, but I wasn't that kind of asshole.

I stood to my feet and sent Jen a flirtatious smirk. "Good talking to you," I said, and she slowly nodded, a bit of a blush flooding her cheeks.

"You, too." I nodded and walked away, feeling the daggers Annie was throwing at me with her gaze, as I walked off, sipping my beer.

This was going to be a long evening if Annie and her husband didn't leave soon.

Chapter 4

Jen

I watched Xander walk away from me and a big part of me wanted to tell these people to fuck off. I was enjoying talking to him. It felt like he understood me. I had never met anyone who understood me like that, what it was like growing up in my dad's shadow.

A small part of me wanted to stay away from him, but a bigger part of me wanted to latch onto him for the understanding he offered. It was a relief, and I told myself that was all it was. Maybe I was in denial, but I craved what Xander had given me in the two minutes we had been talking.

That girl, Keyanna, had run him off and a part of me wanted to punch her in her stomach for that. I would much rather have his company than some woman who thought it was okay to run off one of my cousin's guests at my cousin's party. I was biting my tongue though. I didn't want to start something that came back on Liam. He had been so good to me.

"Key, get off Xander's case," Sally spoke up in her sweet voice. "He's not here to cause trouble." The black girl rolled her eyes before smirking at me.

"My name is Key, and this is my husband, Zane. You're Liam's cousin, right? Liam is such a sweetheart." I slowly nodded.

"Yeah, what's your problem with Xander?" I asked, and Sally gave me a look to say that I had opened up a can of worms. Key took a seat at the edge of my lounger and placed her hand on her belly.

"He tried to kill my husband," she said, bluntly, and I didn't react. There was only one thought going through my mind at that moment.

"What did he do?" I asked, and Key looked surprised.

"Um, excuse me?" She acted like I had offended her, but I didn't give a shit. If you are going to start gossiping about shit like that, you better be ready to get the shit thrown back on yourself.

"If he tried to kill your husband, he probably did something to cause that reaction from Xander. He's a biker, after all. Retaliation is in his blood. So what did your husband do?" That was all it took for the bitchy black woman to stand up and stomp off with her head held high. I smirked triumphantly as Sally followed after her.

"That was so awesome!" A group of three women that I remembered vaguely from the biker bar came and sat around me. All three were white girls. One had strawberry blonde hair and the other two had black hair, but one was cut short and the other was long.

"What do you mean?" I asked, and the blonde laughed.

"We've been waiting for someone to put Keyanna in her place for a year. That girl is such a bitch." I slowly nodded.

"Yeah, I caught that." They grinned at me.

"I'm Laura, by the way," the blonde said. She gave off this sweet, college girl vibe mixed with a sense that she went through hell in the past. "This is

Carrie." She pointed to the girl with short black hair. "And this is Danica." She completed the introductions, and I smirked.

All three of them were stunningly beautiful, much more healthy looking than the whores back in my chapter. How was that possible? Was Xander giving them something that my dad hadn't given the property back home?

"Hi. You guys were at the bar, right?" They nodded. "What is her deal anyway?" I asked, and they looked at me confused. "Why is she so against Xander?" Danica laughed.

"Keyanna dated Xander," she explained, and I felt a bit of a green-eyed monster creeping up. Damn. It was none of my business who he had dated. Calm down, Jen!

"Really?" They nodded. Was that Xander's type? Was he into dark-skinned girls like Keyanna or did he not have a real physical type? He could be pansexual for all I knew. I didn't know Xander very well.

"Yeah, skank fucked herself. She screwed around on him with her hubby. What did she expect him to do? Shake the asshole's hand?" Carrie said, and I nodded.

"What did he do?" I asked, curiously.

"Shot him." That didn't even faze me.

"That's it?" I was shocked that Xander hadn't done worse to him. They looked at me amazed.

"What do you mean?"

"I've seen way worse just from looking at a man's woman. My dad literally

34

cut the dick off my first boyfriend." I sipped my Jack, and they looked at me like I had just stumped them.

"What? Seriously?" Danica asked, looking a bit sick.

"Yeah. Xander went easy on that guy." I took a drink of my whiskey and caught Xander looking at me, sending me a wink, before he jumped into the pool. "And she should've expected some retaliation. He's a biker, raised in the life. I don't see it as Xander did anything wrong," I said, shrugging.

Why was I defending Xander? Sure, he shot a guy who stole his girl. He didn't kill him or beat him to a bloody pulp, but why was I jumping to his defense? He was a grown man. He didn't need me to fight his battles.

I knew the answer, but refused to admit it.

"Excuse me, girls." I needed a break before I lost my shit in front of everyone. I slipped off my lounger and walked over to the pool house. I caught a look at Xander as he jumped out of the pool— drenched, every inch of his tempting body covered in water. He ran his fingers through his hair, sloshing water down his body from the strands.

I was so fucking screwed.

I tried to appear casual as I walked over to my destination and started my freak out beyond the safety of its door. I leaned back against the seashell wallpaper and put pressure on my burning pussy, molten hot lust betraying me, by rubbing my thighs together. No, I wouldn't touch myself. That would be like telling myself that my desire for Xander was okay. It wasn't at all, even if we did have this connection to each other.

First off, he was now my boss. The Black Stallions controlled the bar I was going to be working at.

Secondly, I refused to become a whore. Which is what happened when you messed with a biker. You became property of that gang for anyone to fuck, and no matter how talented his dick might be, it wasn't worth that.

No, I would not yield. I wouldn't give into Xander Davenport.

Zappacosta's *Overload* started to play through the speakers, and it kept me on edge. The door creaked open, and Xander walked through the door, his dark eyes landing on me. His body was tense, as he walked over to me with the gait of a predator, confidence in his stride and lust in his eyes.

"Shouldn't you be partying?" My voice shook from my need. I needed to get away from Xander before I pushed off his bottoms and took his thick throbbing shaft in my mouth. There was too much at risk for me to be losing control of myself right then, less than a couple of hours after I first saw him.

He smirked with a lustful look in his eyes, his eyes raking up and down my body, undressing me with those hazel eyes. Maybe I should've opted for a one-piece and a cover up. Maybe even a blanket.

Him looking at me like that was making the situation even worse. My slit was pulsating, completely soaked, and my walls were vibrating with desire.

"Yeah, well, I have a bit of a confession. I didn't come here for the party." The insinuation didn't go unnoticed by me. He came for me.

"You should stop right there." I gave a half-warning. I couldn't even convince myself to give him the same treatment as the dufus from the clubhouse. He stopped walking for a moment, thinking, then continued his journey to me.

"I don't think you want me to, Jen." He leaned over me and I could feel the heat coming off his body as he stared at me. "I'm pretty sure you don't want me to walk back out that door."

"Cocky much?" I knew he wasn't, but it was the only comeback I could come up with on the drop of a hat. I needed to clear my brain of my lust for this man. He was the one I could never have. I would never let myself give in to him. Never.

"I've seen you watching me, Jen. Your eyes scan every inch of my body and settle on my dick just a bit longer than a curious stare. You want me." My eyes met his, and I couldn't block out the desire in my eyes. I knew he could see it. This was only going to end badly. "Admit it, babe. You want me just as bad as I want you." Then his hand touched my hip, firmly yet still with a gentle grasp. The kind of touch that takes control and guides you in a way that leaves you yearning for more. Mmm, his strong, warm, calloused hand on my skin. The moan slipped out before I could stop it, and he smirked triumphantly. "Say it, Jen." The lion in him thought he had this lamb right in his grasp, but he had another thing coming. There was only one thing I could think to say to save myself from this tragedy.

"I'm not a whore." His eyes snapped from my mouth up to my eyes, studying me. "I'm not going to be one either. I grew up in this thing. I know exactly what happens, and I'm not becoming that woman. If I were to say I want you, that's what happens, so I'm not going to admit to something like that." I spit it out. It was hard to do. All I ever said was that I didn't fuck bikers. I never explained why I distanced myself.

"There is one thing you should know about me, Jen." He bent down and ran his tongue along my earlobe seductively. Fuck, that was one of my sensitive spots. I whimpered, biting my lip. He ran his thumb over my nipple, and I moaned. They were already hard from my arousal. "I don't share," he whispered into my ear, and my eyes snapped open. What did that mean exactly? Did that mean I wouldn't become a house mouse just because of us? "This can be our little secret, for now, beautiful," he said, then kissed and sucked on my neck, pressing his hard cock against my stomach. My toes curled a bit from the contact.

I lost myself to the sensations, his hands on my ass, his mouth leading down toward my chest, his flesh under my hands, his erection stabbing me through his trunks.

"Xander," I whimpered his name, and he returned to his full stature. He took my face in his hands and pressed his mouth to mine for a deep, full-bodied, passionate kiss. A breathy moan slipped into his mouth as his tongue battled with mine.

"Not yet, baby," he whispered as he released the kiss and stared down at me. Not yet? My pussy was pulsating, begging to be filled by him. How could he say not yet? Didn't he say he wanted me? Sure, I wanted to preserve myself, but he said he didn't share. "Later," he whispered, then kissed me again. This time, I clung to him, and I felt a rush of heat flood my body. It took my last thread of self-control not to tear down his bottoms. "Are you done hiding in here now?" he whispered playfully, and I slowly shook my head.

"I needed some privacy." I downplayed it. I needed his dick inside of me, and I needed it really bad.

"Okay. I'll leave you to it." Then, he turned and strolled out.

I raced back into the bedroom of the pool house and quickly pushed off my bottoms. There was no way I would survive the next couple of hours if I didn't get rid of this tension.

I laid on the bed and played with my clit vigorously, begging for a release, but it was holding out. Goddamn it! What was I doing wrong? Why wouldn't the tension leave? Maybe I wasn't relaxed enough for it to come.

Suddenly, my hand was pushed away, and I snapped my eyes open to see Xander was back and shoving his face in my pussy.

What. The. Fuck!

I didn't even try to push him back. I flung my body back on the bed and moaned loudly from the swipe of his barbell-pierced tongue against my clit. God, that felt so good.

"Mmm, you taste so good." He held my thighs apart as he ate up my core, teasing my clit then shoving his tongue past my slit. I cried out in ecstasy. I was going to orgasm soon. I could feel it.

I palmed his hair as he sucked on my clit, and I fucking mewled from how good he was at eating my pussy.

I was about to come. I was right on the edge of it when…

"Jen? Are you in here?" Oh, no! Liam!

Stifling a moan, I pushed Xander's head away as he snapped his gaze to the hall where the voice was coming from.

"Yeah, I just have a headache is all. Go back to your party." I tried to keep my voice level as I covered between my legs. I hurried to grab my bottoms.

"Are you sure? I can get you some Tylenol." I felt him edging toward the door, and I panicked.

"Yeah, I'm sure. I already took something. Go have fun." Xander seemed a little on edge, too, and I was tempted to make him hide, but there was nowhere to hide him. The bathroom was in the hall.

"Alright. Ring me if you need anything." I was able to sigh a breath of relief as I listened to the door closing. That was a close one, and it was exactly what I needed for my arousal to hideaway.

Chapter 5

Xander

I wasn't surprised that Jen rushed me out of the back door of the pool house as soon as Liam left. She needed this thing to be kept quiet and I could respect that.

She was afraid of becoming what her uncle tried to force her to be. That wasn't what she wanted for herself. She didn't know that the same rules didn't apply to me. That was why I kept Annie away from the clubhouse when we were seeing each other. I didn't like to share. The others might be okay with it and, sure, if it was just a casual fuck, I didn't mind handing the girl off to one of my men. Jen wasn't a casual fuck, but damn, if eating her pussy didn't near make me bust a nut in my trunks. I needed to fuck her, but I was a patient man. My balls, on the other hand, weren't.

Jen waited half an hour before coming out, and by then, everyone was getting ready for another game of pool volleyball. This time, I was in on it. I needed something to preoccupy myself from the throbbing of my balls.

"Jen!" Danica called out from the other side of the net. Danica was one of the house mouses. Jen waved back at her. "Play with us! It'll be fun!" she begged, from where she perched on Trip's back.

"Um, sure. Sounds fun." Jen responded as she sauntered over to the water's edge. Her eyes found mine, and I winked at her.

"We get Jen!" Liam said, from my side, and she looked reluctant. She briskly stepped into the pool and took her spot in front of me.

The game started, and she was pretty distracted by me behind her. It was rather amusing to see her squirming from my presence.

It was our serve, and I lobbed the ball which Trip saved. Jen seemed to get out of her funk and leaped up, spiking the ball as soon as it made it past the net which caused it to crash down on the other teams side of the water. Liam cheered and Jen did a bit of a victory dance which was rather sexy before doing a high-five with her cousin.

"That's the game!" Liam whooped, and I lifted Jen onto my shoulders while she shrieked. I knew she was a bit nervous since the last time I was this close to her she was holding my mouth to her pussy.

"Who's up for some chicken?" I asked, and Danica shrieked.

"Us! We want to play!" Trip lifted her onto his shoulders as the net was brought down. "You're going down, Jen," Danica joked, and Jen laughed.

"Right back at ya."

"Be careful there, Dani. My cousin is one bad bitch," Liam joked, before sitting on the edge of the pool. "She has made stronger women cry." This time, he was being serious, and Jen laughed.

"I'll go easy on her," Jen joked, and Danica looked plenty determined.

"Ready, set, chicken!" Drill did the count down, and then Jen and Danica were pulling and pushing at each other. Everyone was cheering for either of the girls, and I caught sight of Annie scowling at us. Well, she could go to hell. I was having fun with Jen.

"I've had too much to drink!" Danica objected right before she fell into the water. Jen was laughing, and I decided to rub the side of my face against the inside of her thigh. She gasped and fell back off my shoulders, tumbling into the water. I laughed, and everyone stared at me surprised. She broke the surface laughing before she scowled at me.

"Did you just bite me?" I slowly shook my head.

"Don't blame me. You fell off just because my beard touched your leg," I challenged her, and she splashed me with water.

"You have some balls, little lady," Domino, the treasurer, said from a lounge. "That's the boss you're splashing at." She sent him a glare before she splashed me again.

"Do not tickle me!" I took the challenge by grabbing her and running my fingers along her gut and legs. "Xander, stop it!" She kept laughing and fighting against me as all eyes settled on us.

"Don't tell me not to tickle you," I whispered, huskily in her ear, and my hand slipped down and cupped her soft peach in my hand. I knew no one could tell I wasn't tickling her as she calmed down her laughter.

I could see that everyone knew I had my eye on Jen, and many of my men stopped looking at us. They knew the drill. If I claimed a woman like Jen, they were to back the fuck off.

"I can't stop thinking about how sweet you taste. I want to eat you up all over again, wrap my tongue around your little clit," I whispered, seductively in her ear, and she slowly pulled away. She knew she had been in my arms a tad

42

too long for people not to know there was something between us.

Even if it wasn't confirmed, everyone had their suspicions, including Liam.

"I think I need a drink," Jen said and climbed out of the pool. I watched her, as she wrapped a towel around herself and disappeared into the house.

"Serious, Xan?" Liam looked pissed.

"What?"

"Leave Jen alone. She's not one of your girls." Liam wasn't in my close circle like Bruce was. He didn't know about my preferences, so I let that slide. Plus, I didn't think Jen would appreciate it if I attacked her cousin.

"Chill out, man." I didn't even deny that I wanted her, and he caught it. I could see it on his face.

"I, for one, like Jen," Laura said, in her soft voice. "She's a bit scary, but a cute kind of scary. Is it true about what she says about her dad?" she asked Liam, who looked at her like she grew another head.

"What about her dad?"

"Well, she said he chopped a guy's dicks off for going near her. Is that true?" she asked Liam, who went pale.

"Wait, what?" Yeah, I remembered that story. Everyone in the gang knew how much of a bad ass Trapper was. "Why would she tell you that?"

"It was just in explaining why she thought Xander went easy on Keyanna's husband when he shot him." Wait, she said what? Did she even know what happened?

"Did you tell her what happened?" I asked. When Laura looked at me, I saw it. The same look she always gave me. The heartbreaking sadness. Fuck, I hated that.

"Keyanna did that bit. I just explained why it happened, and she pretty much just shrugged it off saying you went easy on Zane. She said she had seen way worse happen just for someone looking at someone else's woman. She thinks Keyanna is lucky you didn't do worse than shoot the fucker. Jen does not like Keyanna at all, another reason I like her." Laura had Liam distracted for a bit, which was normal.

I knew Liam had a thing for Laura. It had been obvious since the day the two of them met but nothing ever happened. It wasn't allowed to unless I gave the go ahead which I hadn't. Laura was good at keeping Liam preoccupied with her authentic sweet girl vibe and outgoing personality.

I slipped out of the pool during the distraction. I found my jeans and pulled out my phone. Luckily, I had gotten Jen's number from Bruce, so I didn't have to chase after the girl.

I liked that girl even more now than I did before.

I wrote up a text to Jen.

Me: Are you alright?

Jen: Who is this?

Me: Xander. Did I embarrass you, babe?

Jen: No. I don't get embarrassed.

I smirked from that. I bet I could find some way to do that.

44

Me: So if I went up to your cousin and told him I ate you out in the pool house, you'd be cool with that?

Jen: Don't you dare! I'll kick your ass!

Me: Kinky, I dare you to try.

Jen: Don't tempt me.

Me: Where are you? Are you going to avoid me for the rest of the night?

Jen: Maybe. Are you going to keep trying to get in my pants?

Me: You weren't wearing pants, just a sexy as fuck bikini.

Jen: Xander!

I could practically feel her glaring at her phone, and I grinned. I liked getting under her skin.

Me: I'm not trying to get in your pants. I went to see what was taking you so long and saw you struggling to get off. I wanted to help, and your pussy tasted so good. Go ahead. Sue me for finding you so damn irresistible.

Jen: Maybe I will. You're enough of an ass. I might actually win.

Me: I'm not an ass just because I know you want me.

Jen: Conceited, too. You are making your case even worse.

Me: What case?

Jen: The reasons why I'm not going to fuck you. You are just stacking them up.

Wait, she was making a list? Why was she so against this? I wasn't looking to fuck her right now, but at some point, yeah. I knew she liked me. It was obvious when we were talking, kissing, or she was threatening me. We both liked each other, and she was holding back. What was it about me or this that scared her?

Me: What are the reasons you have so far?

Jen: Number one, you're a biker.

What? Seriously? Does she have a problem with me being a biker? She was a fucking biker's daughter. That made no sense.

Me: Why is that a reason?

Jen: Because I won't be a house mouse, so no fucking bikers. Sorry, not sorry.

Me: You do know I run my chapter different than the others, right?

Jen: How so?

Me: I'm the president, Jen. Just because you fuck me doesn't mean you become property. Those girls sign up for this shit. They take a pledge and know exactly what they are up for and what is expected of them. Other places, sure, that might be the case, but not here.

Me: Secondly, no one touches what is mine. My men know that.

I waited for her response, and it took a while.

Jen: Let me guess. You think I'm yours?

I smirked at that answer. I could just imagine the sassy look on her face.

You can bet your gorgeous ass on it, babe.

Chapter 6

Jen

My mind had been swirling all evening, lying in my bed. I wasn't drunk. I barely had two drinks, but Xander was messing with my head.

Only a blind man wouldn't see how much we wanted each other. I was lusting and so was he. He answered some of my questions, but it was that one text that he sent that was messing with my head.

I'd like you to be.

Just five words. He was admitting that he wanted me to be his. I kept trying to deflect it in my head, but I couldn't use my desire to not be a biker bitch as a shield. I got it confirmed by Danica that those girls took a pledge, and none of them were forced into it.

Danica knew something about the reasons for Xander taking away the forcefulness of it from the gang. No girls had been raped or forced into being whores since Xander started his reign over the chapter, and I had to wonder why. No one would say.

Did something happen to him or someone he cared about?

I liked Xander, a lot, and that made this dangerous. I didn't want to be one of those women who let themselves fall for a man and then had their heartbroken. I had been able to avoid it so far, but was it at the age of twenty-seven that I would finally get the first blow to my heart? Was Xander Davenport my kryptonite?

I wished I could talk to Meg. She was one of my best friends growing up, and I had to cut ties when I ran. I couldn't take the chance that my uncle would use her to find me. She was safer if she didn't know anything, and so was I.

I knew what Meg would say anyway. She would tell me to take a chance with Xander and offer my heart. She would say it is better to have loved and lost than never to have loved at all. Damn. I could hear her saying it in my head.

I was thinking of going for a walk to clear my head. I had already gotten dressed in some jeans, riding boots, a long sleeve thermal, and my dad's crew jacket. I was going to grab my phone when my bedroom door opened, and there he was.

"Xander," I muttered, surprised, and he smirked at me. He wasn't in his bathing suit anymore. Jeans, a black long-sleeve shirt, and his crew vest. God, he was so handsome. I loved the scruff on his face and how it complimented his scar and bad boy look.

"Hey, beautiful." He slipped inside, and I stared at him with disbelief.

"What are you doing up here?" I was getting a bit suspicious, but I pushed it down.

"I'm about to head out. Liam is drunk near the pool with his band. Do you want to come along?" He nodded in the direction of the driveway, and I took a minute to think.

Xander hadn't done anything wrong. Even when he grabbed me in the pool, his hand felt so good. I was getting worked up again just thinking about it. His hands. His mouth. His tongue. Shit. I was wet again.

My inner Meg voice was right. I didn't know what would happen with Xander until I went for it, and I would eventually do it anyway. He had such power over me.

"Where to?" I asked, and he grinned.

"You'll see. Come on," he urged and extended his hand to me. I took it quickly, and he grinned at me as he led me downstairs. The party had mostly come inside except for Liam and his band. They were still on the porch, but everyone else was in the living room, laughing and drinking.

"Jen!" Danica waved at me from her seat on Trip's lap, and I smirked.

She was a sweet girl. We could be friends for sure. I was curious about one thing. What was up with her and Trip? Danica was clinging to him all evening, but she was unclaimed. Was there something going on there? I wasn't sure. Maybe Trip was just her favorite of the guys. I could understand that. Trip was handsome with his short blonde hair, smokey eyes, and toned physique. It was no surprise that Danica would attach herself to him.

"We're heading out. Don't wreck Liam's house," Xander shouted out an order, and everyone's eyes fell to his hand around mine. The men all looked away, but the girls gave me a big, congratulatory grin.

"Have fun, Jen!" Laura cheered, and maybe, I was a tad embarrassed that everyone knew that I was, kind of, Xander's girl. We'd see what happened.

Xander guided me to his bike that was parked down the street. He hopped on, and I got on behind him, gripping my hands on his waist.

50

"Have you been on a bike before?" I laughed at his question.

"Since before I could walk. I'm more comfortable on a bike than a car. Do you have any idea how many more cars get in accidents than motorcycles? It's a scary thought." He chuckled softly from my response.

"I concur, babe." Then, we were off.

Xander drove for about an hour. We went down some winding dirt roads through the thick cover of trees until we got to what looked like some farmland.

There was a decently sized cabin at the front of the property aged with dents and discoloration to the wood and a red barn covered in rust that was closed up. The place was mostly deserted except for some pigs and a cornfield.

"Where are we?" The place was peaceful. It wasn't calming or serene. A normal person would've been scared off by the vibe the place gave off. I got the sense that some sinister things had gone down there and that didn't worry me. The disturbing nature of the land brought a sense of calm to me. I felt at home there.

Xander parked the bike next to the blue Silverado I recognized from the bar, and we settled down on the top of an old wooden picnic table near the cabin covered in carvings into the wood and blood stains. The table was almost completely red like Xander had used blood bags to stain it that color.

"My place," he explained, and I slowly nodded. "It used to be the original private clubhouse when my dad was alive." I watched him as he stared at the barn. "It's a pretty freaky place, huh?" he joked, and I slowly shook my head.

"Not to me. It's a bit relaxing. It's got this vibe to it. One that says something bad happened here. My dad used to take me places like this all the time. He'd play a little game with it. Guess How Many People Died Here." He chuckled.

"Damn. Are we fucked up or what?"

"No, it's our upbringing. Who doesn't get fucked up growing up in a biker club?" He slowly nodded.

"Touche. Explains why my little brother wants nothing to do with it. It freaked my ex out when I told her that I didn't want kids. Who wants to bring a kid into this shit when you've seen the kind of shit we have?" A little more insight into Xander than I expected.

He didn't want children which was a bit of a clash. I did. Someday. Maybe in another five years.

"I think both of our parents just did it wrong. They weren't careful enough. I think it's possible to raise a kid in this and not screw them up." I shrugged, nonchalantly.

"Maybe. I mean, Bruce might have a chance there. Maybe he's actually doing it right." I looked at Xander, confused.

"I thought Bruce was just like a brother?" I asked, and he chuckled.

"Bruce is a complicated situation. It's hard to explain. This is actually where Bruce became a part of the organization." He motioned to everything, and I nodded.

"Out here?"

"Yeah."

"What's the story there?" His face lost its expression as he pulled out a cigarette and lit it.

"Sally was married before Bruce. It was over ten years ago. The guy she had been married to was harassing her. I didn't ask questions. I had a rule out for a while. If Bruce Mayes needs something, do it. No questions asked. When he went to my brother with his problem, Austin came to me." I slowly nodded.

"Sally's pregnancy was rough. Her life was put in danger by the smallest amount of stress, and her ex stressed her out. Most guys would've done anything to protect their girl and their kids, but Bruce had always been this squeaky clean kid. He was a protective little shit, but not a dark person," he explained, then looked at me like he thought I might stop the story. No, I wanted to hear it. Maybe it made me dark, but I liked stories like this.

"Keep going," I egged him on and laced my fingers through his. He gave me a cute little smirk before looking back at the barn.

"The situation was complicated because the guy was also his brother-in-law. My guys had to wait until Bruce's sister wasn't around to grab him. They brought him here, and we all waited for Bruce to get here. When Bruce arrived, I saw a completely different side to him than I have ever seen. I can name three times in my life where I saw someone take their time like that. He made a lot of my men cringe. I think Trip might've puked." I nodded along with what he was saying.

"Well, some people would go to great lengths to protect the people they love." He smirked at me from that, and I flushed.

"His uncle was my dad's first VP until he passed away. I gave him his uncle's crew vest. He's not a biker, but he's one of us. He's like a brother. The whole chapter sees him that way."

"You should. Sometimes the darkest shit bonds people." He took a drag off his cigarette before throwing it on the ground.

"You can say that again. You know, you're a bit wise for your age." I rolled my eyes. For my age?

"What am I supposed to be?" I then turned to him and got my best teenie bopper voice. "Oh, my god, Xander. That is just so gross. I'm out. I'm heading to the club now." He laughed at my crack on my generation.

"Real cute," he uttered between cackles, and I smirked.

"If I ever start acting like that, you have my permission to shoot me," I joked, and he squeezed my hand. "Or better yet, send me back to the desert. I'm sure my uncle would love to do it himself," I mumbled, and he looked at me curiously.

"What is his problem with you?"

"I'm guessing Bruce told you my story?" I answered his question with another.

"Not quite sure how much of it. It seemed pretty rough." I nodded and pulled my lips into a tight line. I had told the story already, but it was harder with it being Xander. I didn't want him to think I was broken by what happened. I wasn't. I was fine. He deserved to know though.

"The crew had been on my dad's back to name someone to take over after him. He avoided it for a while. I'm not sure why. I think he just didn't want to think about what would happen to everyone once he was gone or just the idea of him dying. He wouldn't talk about it with me," I explained, and he nodded. "My dad talked to me about a lot of shit that bothered him, but not that. It even surprised me when he announced that he wanted me to take over for him." He didn't say anything, just listened.

"You know just as well as I do that he was asking for trouble. The whole chapter broke into an uproar over it. People were split. A few thought it might be a good idea, changing the club's culture. Most of them didn't feel that way though. Some thought I had brainwashed him, but I never wanted to take over. I even told my dad that after he made the announcement. He said he didn't have any sons and wasn't going to let it leave the family. 'It has to be you, Jennifer.' That's what my dad said.

"My uncle and the parts of the club loyal to him executed my dad for naming me the heir. It sucked, losing him. My mom died ten years ago, and my dad was all I had left, other than my uncles and cousins and Liam, but I understood why Crack did it. My dad lost his mind, and Crack saw it as him risking the club's future.

"Crack called me to the club's bar for a meeting. I wasn't sure what it was for. I went anyway. Half the crew pretty much ambushed me. I ran and now here I am." I skipped over my uncle commanding my attempted gang-rape. It wasn't necessary. "Crack thinks he can't completely take over the chapter if I'm alive, so he put a hit out on me. As long as I stay far away from there, I should be safe. He doesn't know about Liam, so he has no reason to look here for me." I shrugged and slipped off my jacket, setting it in my lap. He looked at me curiously, his eyes hazy.

"Is that your dad's crew jacket?" I slowly nodded.

"It's all I have left of him," I admitted and lifted the locket from under my shirt. "This is all I have left of my mom. She gave it to me right before she died. My dad pretty much killed her without pulling the trigger. It's kind of sad, really." He squeezed my hand with a frown across his face.

"What do you mean?" he asked, with the softest voice I had ever heard from a full-grown man.

"She killed herself," I admitted, and his eyes widened. "She didn't know my dad was a biker when she met him. He kept that pretty well hidden, and his crew as well, until she was pregnant with me. Then, he dropped it all on her. Even though he had her, he was constantly screwing around on her with the girls, which is why I'm an only child. She said as long as he was fucking around on her, she refused to fuck him. That argument didn't always end well for her, and I had to see it a lot." He wrapped an arm around my shoulder, as I sighed. "He broke her heart constantly for seventeen years. She couldn't take it anymore, so she killed herself. I found her, and my dad didn't bat an eyelash at it." I tried to shrug, but I knew I wasn't fooling him. My mom was the one person I ever loved and wanted to save, but I couldn't. My face fell, and I felt his arms move around me supportively.

"Jen..." I slowly shook my head.

"It was a long time ago."

"That doesn't matter. That was your mom."

"That's what it's like being raised in the club, Xander. You know that. Some people can handle it. Others can't. My mom was just one of the people that couldn't. Shit happens." I tried to brush it off, but he didn't let me.

"Jen, don't downplay it. My mom went through some shit, too. My mom wasn't married to my dad. My mom was a mouse."

"What?" He slowly nodded.

"Yup. My mom got knocked up. She got a DNA test done, and it proved who my father was, but it just was dumb luck that my dad was the president. Austin has a different father. His dad was... was Bruce's uncle." I nodded him along. "Growing up as the kid of a mouse isn't quite that glamorous since after having me, she was still expected to... service... the crew. Even with me and Austin in the room. Sometimes, she would just get dragged off into a room and come out half an hour later beaten to a bloody pulp." Oh. My. God. "You want to know why I run my organization different than the others? That's why." That made me look at Xander in a different light. He wasn't a monster like other bikers. He had a heart, and he cared about others genuinely.

That made it even harder to guard my heart.

"Um, I think I should go." I needed to get away from him, or I would be in worse trouble than I already was. I could feel myself starting to linger on the edge, and I needed to pull myself back.

I grabbed my jacket and started walking toward his bike with my emotions starting to get the best of me. Why the hell couldn't I guard myself against Xander? My walls just came down around him, and I couldn't push him away. Damn it. He was the one who drove me out here. I had no idea how to get back to Liam's house.

"Why do you keep doing that?" I stopped when I heard his voice from behind me. Tears were clouding my eyes, and I was fighting with everything in me. "Why do you keep pulling back and running off? I know you feel the same way as me. I can see and feel it, Jen. Why the hell are you running from me?" I turned to him with frustration.

"Because I can't become my mom!" He looked hurt by what I said, and it sent a pain through my gut. "I've survived twenty-seven years by doing everything not to get in the position she was in. I don't date bikers, I don't do relationships longer than a couple of weeks, and I definitely don't let myself get knocked up by some guy I don't even know. I don't give my heart away, and that's the way I like it. It's what I'm comfortable with. Not this, Xander. This is not comfortable for me. I don't know anything about you, and for some reason, I…" I had to cut myself off before I started crying. I couldn't

57

cry. I wouldn't. I was a strong, independent woman. Why the hell was he getting to me?

"You what?" He strolled over to me as I cringed, trying to get my emotions in check, but they wouldn't calm down. "You want this. You want to feel like this, and you want me." I gulped, and went to object, but Xander kissed me, pulling me close against him.

It wasn't one of desire, but one of caring and devotion and determination. I felt myself losing this battle of wills and, like I always knew, Xander was winning. He would always win this battle.

Chapter 7

Xander

She didn't want to admit how she felt and that was okay. Her body was doing all the talking for her, and it was saying a lot. A full conversation was being had between my body and hers.

She wanted this. She wanted me. It was an undeniable spark, and now, I got the reason for it. We could both sense that we understood each other in a way no one else had, a way no one else could. While I tried to deal with my childhood by bettering the organization that caused it, she did it by trying to distance herself from it, but she knew she couldn't deny this.

Us.

It made no sense to her. Hell, I was struggling to understand it, but I was catching on pretty fast.

We stumbled into my room, and she pushed my vest over my shoulders while still kissing me passionately. I groaned as I felt her nails scratch along my abs from where she snuck her hands under my shirt. I took her face in my hands and deepened the kiss, which she made a weird noise at. I loved it when she made that sound. It was the mixture of the mewl of a cat in heat and the growl of a tiger. It was delicious.

I yanked her thermal up her chest, and she lifted her arms in consent to this. I tossed it to the side and kissed down her neck, growling into her ear.

I was so glad she was all mine.

She forced me to sit on the edge of the bed and straddled my waist, kissing me again. I was quick to undo her bra, and she threw the material away, revealing her gorgeous, full voluptuous chest. I bent my head down and kissed, licked, sucked at her erect, pink nipples. She groaned, as she dug her fingers through my hair. She was thoroughly enjoying the sensation of the barbell in my tongue against her sensitive areola.

"Xander, I want you," she whispered to me, and warmth flooded me from her confession. I already knew she did, but to hear it was a whole different thing. It was a rush.

"Fuck... please, tell me you're on birth control." I came up for air before going back to her tits.

"God, Xan... yes, I get the shot like clockwork." She pushed up my shirt, and I took the hint. I tossed away my shirt and pulled her bare flesh flush against mine as I kissed her, flipping us over.

She laid limp against my bed, as I took in the sight of her. I had fucked plenty of girls, none of them I had ever brought to my cabin. Not even Laura came here. It was my solace, and now, Jen was in it. I had let her invade my space, and it didn't bother me with it being her.

"What's the matter?" she asked, concern on her face.

"Nothing. You're just so beautiful," I said before kissing her again. She moaned, and I felt her hands working at my belt.

"Please, Xan," she was begging for it. Who was I to deny her?

I pulled myself back and undid her jeans before pulling them and her panties down her legs together. She lifted her ass for me and there she was, in my bed. Naked. Completely fucking naked for me. I fantasized about this since I first saw her, and the reality made the fantasy seem like an Etch-A-Sketch drawing. Her body was perfect, no scars of stretch marks. Her skin was flawless everywhere.

Was I dreaming? How could a woman this perfect want me? I didn't think I would ever understand it.

She sat up and worked on my jeans. She used her dainty little feet to push down my jeans, and my dick sprung out like a jack-in-the-box. I could see the shock on her face, and I chuckled at that. Yup, I got that every time a girl saw my dick for the first time. The piercing shocked a lot of people more than my size did.

"Oh, my god. You have your dick pierced?" I chuckled and kicked off my jeans.

"All for your pleasure, babe. Enjoy it because that shit hurt like a bitch when I first had it done." She laughed at what I said.

"No shit! Isn't that the most sensitive part of the male body?" She was still snickering with amusement.

"Second most sensitive," I said, then cut off her retort by kissing her. She gave up the conversation and scratched at my back as I nudged her legs apart. It felt so good, her nails digging into my skin, her smooth legs rubbing against my hips, her soft, moist pussy against the mushroom of my dick.

I teased her slit with my cock, and she moaned.

"Put it in my pussy, Xan." Fuck. I was starting to like the way that nickname sounded on her lips.

"You don't want me to tease you a bit, baby?" I was messing with her, and she knew it.

"You've teased me enough for one day." I chortled from her joke, and she kissed along my cheek before softly running her lips along the scar across my eye. That thing was so sensitive, and her touch was so sensual. Most were uncomfortable with my scar, but she wasn't. She didn't shy away from it. She didn't ask about it either.

"Jen," I mumbled her name, as she softly ran her fingers through my hair, affectionately teasing my scalp.

"Xander, please." I pressed my forehead to hers and pressed into her. Slow and easy. Shit. She was tight, fitting me like a glove. My jaw slacked with pleasure, and I pressed completely into her.

"Fuck," I groaned, as she clung to me. "You're so tight. It feels so good." She whimpered and nodded.

"Keep going, Xan. Make me yours."

Shit, baby. You're already mine. Do I need to remind you? I thrusted against her, and her pussy oozed her arousal around me, as she dug her nails deeper into my flesh.

She was moaning and whimpering as I quickened my pace, working my cock harder into her. I gave it to her deeper and harder as she cried out in pleasure, nails digging into my back. She broke the skin, but I didn't mind. I liked the pain.

CHAPTER 7

We didn't need words. Our bodies were doing all the talking. Hers was chatting nonstop and mine was listening, coaxing the chatter from hers.

I groaned and sucked on her neck as I drilled myself into her sexy body.

I didn't know how much longer I could last. I needed to make sure she came before I reached my peak. I teased her clit, and she shook beneath me.

"Xan!" she screamed for me as she squeezed my cock good and hard. Her body was shaking from her release as she clung to me.

That's right, Jen. Let yourself feel good.

I lost my rhythm as my balls tensed, and I groaned.

"I'm gonna come," I groaned as she grabbed my ass, squeezing, begging for me to give it to her. "Fuck, yes!" I growled as I came hard for her. I shot off like a racehorse and nearly collapsed on her from the mind-blowing orgasm she gave me. I hadn't come like that in... well, I couldn't remember the last time it had been like that.

Ecstasy, euphoria, and bliss clouded my mind in a way I hadn't felt in such a long time.

I rolled her with me, and she laid across my chest as I held her close. She didn't speak. She just laid there, rubbing her hand up and down my chest. I had her head tucked under my chin, and I kept going from playing with her hair to rubbing her back.

"Jen?" She hummed her response as I pressed a soft kiss to the top of her head. "I'll never let anything happen to you. I promise." I meant every word. She slowly lifted her head and those sapphire eyes of hers locked with mine, her finger playing with the scruff on my face. She just stared at me, a kaleidoscope of emotions flickered across her face. Sadness. Glee. Rapture. Determination. Apprehension. Desire.

She moved over me and kissed me with passionate zeal, her long hair fanning around us. Then, she took me back inside of her and rode me for over an hour.

* * *

I let out a big yawn as the light poured in through the window, and I looked down at Jen, stuck in a deep sleep beside me. Shallow breaths and an emotionless expression covered her, as I threw my arms around her, holding her close. I had forgotten she stayed the night until I saw her there. A strange pleasure filled me from the reality of her presence. It was something I had never felt. I wasn't sure if I felt uneasy about it or not, but I relaxed with her there.

She burrowed into my embrace, and she let out a soft breath. Maybe she had woken up, but if she did, it was only momentary. She was back asleep in a moment.

I followed her into the land of fantasies and nightmares. Luckily, mine was empty except for the feeling of contentment that surrounded me like a security blanket.

I woke up a couple of hours later to the sensation of Jen wiggling against me. I opened my eyes to see her back pressed against my front, and my hard stem was pressed against her ass.

She was letting out those adorable whimpers of desire, and I groaned.

"Damn, babe. What a way to wake a guy up," I teased as I kissed along her shoulder and kneaded her waist. She felt so good in my arms.

"You're the one who started stabbing my ass with your dick. Do you have any idea how cold that piercing is?" I laughed. She was adorable.

"You weren't complaining last night."

"I didn't have a reason to complain last night. We were fucking. We aren't right now." I smirked at her sassy assessment.

"We need to fix that." She moaned from my aroused whisper. I lifted her leg and slipped my dick in between her legs, teasing her slit with the blossom of my stem. Her flower hummed from the tease, and she shivered.

"Xan, don't tease me." I sucked on her earlobe and gripped tight to the sensitive skin of her thigh. I could feel the muscle tensing and relaxing with each caress of my head on her entrance.

"Are you ready for me, baby?" I whispered in her ear and was encased with the sound of her aroused noises.

"Fuck me, Xan. Fuck me, now," she demanded, with need dripping from her tongue, and I buried myself deep inside her. My stem was gripped tight by her walls, wet and convulsing. She cried out with desire, rapture, and ecstasy sweating out her pores, and I bit into the juncture where her shoulder met her neck. She had a vice grip on me, and it kept tightening more and more with each thrust into her deepening flower.

I buried my face in her sea of chocolate strands and honeysuckle scent, need coursing through my veins. I wanted her, needed her. It was more than just sex, which I hadn't felt in a while. It was scary yet thrilling at the same time.

"Yes, Jen… that pussy… so fucking warm and good… so damn good," I groaned with pleasure, as she turned her head and kissed me. Hmm, she tasted good. She was sweet like honey and fresh vanilla. There was the slightest hint of whiskey on her tongue from the night before, but it wasn't overwhelming. It didn't take away from the honey and vanilla.

"Xander… oh, god." She pulled away, and I slipped out of her warmth. Shock filled me, as she released the kiss. Before I had a chance to address her rejection, she pushed me onto my back and crawled onto me like a sexy panther, slow and predatory. She took my length back inside of her, squealing with pleasure, before taking me in and out of her, bouncing up and down, crying with each movement.

Ecstasy rushed through my body as my hips bucked toward hers, and she pressed her palms on my chest.

"Xan, shit… oh, fuck, yes." She mewled with rapture as her jaw slacked, pleasure across her face. "I'm about to come." I could feel it. She was tightening more and more with each passing second. Her arms were trembling from her impending release. She had a few moments before it would hit.

I sat up and took her in my arms, as I slammed my mouth against hers. I grabbed her ass and fucked her hard, burying myself into her depth repeatedly while she clung to me like a life-preserver.

"Xan, I'm coming. Oh, my fuck!" She came up for air as I kissed along her jaw. She arched toward me, as I increased my pace. Harder… Deeper… Faster… More. I gave her more, relentlessly. I fucked her with everything in me, and she was screaming for more, clinging to me. She was so needy for what I was giving her. This was where my cock needed to be, and she needed this just as much as I did.

"Jen, fuck…" I growled, as she pressed her mouth back against mine.

"Xan, don't stop… give it to me, baby… make me yours." Did she still not understand? By god, I had fucked her into oblivion last night, and she still wasn't grasping it. Did she need me to say it? Maybe she did.

"How can I make you mine when you're already mine, babe?" I grunted, and her eyes met mine with realization and acceptance.

"Yeah, I'm yours, Xan." Then, she kissed me. That was all I needed.

She admitted that she was mine with no resistance or hesitation. It was simple and yet an admission of such dedication. Maybe that was all either of us needed to hear or say to know where we stood. For now, at least.

Chapter 8

Jen

Haerts' *Your Love* vibrated through my earbuds as I gazed at the black walls of the bar that I was now working in.

Last night and this morning felt like a dream. I had sex with Xander, five times. Twice last night and three times this morning. It was passionate, zealous, hypnotizing, rough, alluring sex. It left my body full of a need for more which was new. I never had a desire to go back for more, but Xander was different. He made me feel things I had never allowed myself to feel with another man, and he beckoned them out of me. No matter how much I resisted, I couldn't deny him my heart.

Of course, Liam freaked out when I walked into his house at noon wearing my clothes from the night before. He tried to warn me off of Xander. He was a biker, after all. Biker spelled trouble and considering where I came from, he expected me to avoid Xander Davenport like he had HIV.

If Xander hadn't gotten the reaction from me that he had, I might heed the warning, but I couldn't turn back. I had opened the floodgates and let my emotions free. I couldn't lock them away again. Xander was like me. He was a club offspring, and he understood what it was like growing up the way I had. He didn't look at me like I was crazy, impulsive, or heartless. He just saw me, and he didn't run away.

He was the first guy not to run, and I liked that about him. I didn't scare him just like he didn't scare me. I was just Jen, not the daughter of the insane founding father of the Black Stallions international motorcycle club, not the fugitive running from Crack to escape her death, not the scared little girl who lost all of her family. No, I was only Jen to Xander, and I loved that. I loved being seen as me and that was something I never had. My mom always saw my dad when she looked at me and vice versa. I wasn't a thing of joy for them because of their twisted relationship.

I knew my parents loved me, sure, but that love was tarnished long ago. There was always a 'but' I saw in their eyes.

I love you, sweetheart, but you remind me of my husband who raped me repeatedly and broke my heart on a daily basis by screwing everything that moved. That was what my mom's eyes always said.

My dad's stare was even worse. *I love you, and one day you will do great things, but half of you is the miserable whore who just couldn't take the life of a den mother. She was weak, and you better not be the same, or I'll end you with a flick of my wrist.* Yup, that sounded about right. He said as much a few times when he was drunk.

My love for my mom was unconditional, but my dad, his was a bit more like his for me. *Dad, I love you. I really, truly do, but I wish I had driven my swiss army knife into your kidney long before you killed Mom.* Yup, I had a lot of repressed rage toward my dad.

Now, when it came to Xander 'Gunner' Davenport... there were no exceptions to my affections for him. Xander made me happy just by being himself. I had never felt that before. I wouldn't call it love because it was too soon for that and a scary thought, but I had feelings for Xander. True, deep, raw emotions, and I couldn't send them away once he had opened my eyes to them. He opened my heart that had felt like it was dead for so long.

"Oh, Jen." I pulled out one of my earbuds and paused my music as I turned to Derek, a nice, heavy set black man about ten years older than Xander.

"Yes?"

"Could you be a dear and take the trash out for me? I can finish setting up." Derek's Bar and Grill opened their doors from ten in the morning to ten at night for the public, but after ten, it was club territory.

This was my test run. Derek's waitress had called in sick for the evening, so he had to tend to his customers, and I arrived to help clear the tables and get things set up for the bikers. Derek said it was my job to keep the Black Stallions happy, but I would be done if they weren't satisfied with my service. If the place was clean when he got in at nine in the morning, he would give me some day shifts to earn some tips. He made sure I was aware that I was a Black Stallion's employee for now and that my performance would determine if he was willing to take me on during the other hours.

For now, my hours would depend on how drunk the bikers wanted to get.

"Sure, Mr. Watson. No problem." He hummed and approached me.

"Derek. None of this 'Mr. Watson', pretty lady." Really? God, not this.

"Um, I'd prefer to keep things professional," I said, then grabbed the trash. I ran out the backdoor and groaned as I tossed the trash.

"Was it heavy?" I jumped and turned to see Xander there.

"God, don't sneak up on me like that." I swatted at his arm, and he pulled me into him, kissing me passionately.

"You shouldn't be frowning like that, sweetheart." His voice was like icicles, sharp and cold. Not the warm, caring Xander I was used to.

"Who said I was frowning?"

"Your groan did. What's the matter?" he asked, and my frown returned.

"I'm not going to say. I can deal with my own problems, Xander."

"I know you can. You don't need me or anyone else fighting your battles for you, but I want to know why you seem upset." I sighed in defeat, as his honey hazel eyes stared into mine.

"Men are assholes. Not you, but other men." He chuckled.

"Babe, you don't need to be polite. I know I'm an asshole."

"It's no big deal, Xan. I've dealt with much bigger problems, but Derek was trying to… test out the waters." Not sure if I worded that right for him to understand without saying he tried to see if he could flirt with me.

"Test out the waters? Derek tried to come onto you?" His teeth gritted, and I gently touched his clothed pecs.

"No. I think he was just putting feelers out to see if it would be alright if he did. I shut him down, but still, it was annoying. Do men think with anything other than their penises?" I figured the joke would lighten the blow of 'someone made a move on my woman' which pissed off all bikers. I was right. He laughed.

"Not all of us. You are offending my entire gender, woman."

"Woman? Talk about offending one's gender." He raised an eyebrow at me.

"Female? Girl?... Pussy?" I slapped his chest, and he laughed again. "You know I'm just messing with you."

"I know, but you messing with me doesn't cure the problem of men objectifying me for their pleasure." He gave me that sexy smirk of his that got close to dropping my panties every time he did it. Fuck.

"I have an idea of how to fix that." He had that look in his eyes. The one that said let's fuck, and I knew exactly what plan he had. He wanted us to have sex behind the bar, loud enough that Derek would hear. He would come check on the disturbance and find me and Xander fucking. It was Xander's way of saying back off and that's my girl.

Yup, I was Xander's woman, which meant I also knew when to say exactly what I did in reply.

"Ugh, no!" I turned and stalked off toward the back door.

"It would be fun." He used that teasing voice again, and I flipped him the finger over my shoulder.

"Fuck you!"

"You, too, babe!" I could hear the amusement in his voice as I slipped inside which let me know he wasn't offended by my way of rejecting his offer.

Sure, I loved sex. Loved sex with Xander specifically. Did I want my overweight, clammy-pawed boss to watch Xander fuck me into oblivion? Hell, no. Other people I would be okay with, but I was not looking to lose this job. Sure, if I wasn't working there, I would probably still be coming by with Xander, but I needed the money. I needed this job.

CHAPTER 8

*** ***

It was two in the morning, and the main players of the chapter were in the bar along with Carrie and Laura who I learned were the favorite mouses in the club. Trip favored Danica more than anyone else. I had the feeling that maybe Trip was in love with her. The single men in the chapter would cry if Trip locked her down.

Derek's Bar was nicer than the biker bar. The floors were clean, white tile and all the wooden tables were in perfect condition. The lighting was even better. The bar was completely lit up, not a dark spot in sight.

"So, Jen," Laura slurred a bit as Xander pulled me into his lap, rubbing his hands up my thighs sensually. "Tell me about your cousin." Laura was drunk. She had been chugging those pink, girlie drinks all night, and I think they were all hitting her all at once.

I had no idea why she was suddenly asking about Liam. I was shocked when I got home from Xander's place and found that Laura had stayed there with Liam while I was gone. I knew she was a mouse but apparently, she and my cousin had a little love affair that no one knew about. It had shocked me. There was no reason to be asking about my cousin.

"Liam? What about him?"

"He was just sooo sweet last night. Is he from... Australia, too?" she asked, while leaning against the table. Her eyes seemed to drift between me and Xander like she was waiting on reactions to her line of questioning. Maybe she wasn't drunk after all.

"No. He's from Chicago. My mom's side of the family all lived in Chicago.

My mom was the first to leave. She went on vacation to Sydney and never went back, then Liam moved off to Los Angeles for music gigs then to San Jose. He's been the rhythm guitarist for Mayes for ten years, I think." I gave a bit of information, and she groaned.

"Laura, just ask what you're really looking for," Xander commanded, before sipping on his beer. He sounded a bit irritated.

"Well, is he single?"

"Single? You want to know my cousin's relationship status?" She nodded rapidly, and Crank looked at her baffled. What did it matter? She was already screwing him.

"Bullshit! You thinking of leaving us, sweetheart?" She gave him a challenging look.

"If the right man arises to the challenge..." I laughed at her boldness. Yup, she was plastered. "Liam seems like the kind of man that knows how to treat a woman, in and out of the bedroom." Too much information.

"Fuck me." Crank downed his shot of... tequila? Maybe bourbon? I couldn't remember. Everyone had been switching up their drinks all night. I had been slowly sipping a glass of whiskey.

"Well?" Laura pressed, and I smirked.

"He is very single. I'm not sure if he even does relationships. We didn't talk about that shit until this morning when I got home." Holy shit. Did that just come out of my mouth? I hope they didn't catch that. It's not that I was embarrassed of Xander or being with him. I just didn't want his crew jumping to the conclusion that it was just sex, a hookup, between me and Xander. It wasn't, and we both knew it. Everyone else, I wasn't sure.

"Well, damn," Laura groaned, and I looked over to see Trip and Danica were making out like a horny couple.

"Overprotective family members, am I right?" Crank joked, and I nodded as Xander kissed my neck.

"Liam would be the only one. The rest of my family... is a different story. Well, the only one left anyway," I said, then downed the last of my whiskey that I had been sipping all night. I eyed some club girls doing a striptease on one of the far tables for some bikers, but I noticed Xander's eyes didn't even glance in that direction. They were on me, and he was focused on the conversation.

"That blows," Crank stated, as he lit up a joint and passed it over to me. "You want a toke, sweetheart?" Crank was an older man, close to sixty, maybe a bit older, so I didn't mind the kid name he gave me. Xander had used the same name with me, but with a carnal edge that Crank lacked when he said it.

"Sure, old timer," I joked, and he grinned. I took a hit off the joint, then passed it along to Xander who held onto it for a bit, taking a few drags off it, savoring the high.

"Well, family sucks." He nodded.

"Your parents still around?" Crank asked, a bitter sweetness to his expression. He was remembering his family, probably.

"Nope. My mom passed away ten years ago, and my dad died three weeks ago." Crank frowned.

"Awe, sorry to hear that. It's hard losing your parents."

"You'll learn to humor Crank. He gets sentimental when he drinks," Xander whispered in my ear, and I snickered.

"Not so difficult when you've dreamed of gutting said parent for over a decade." I didn't even realize what had come out of my mouth until Laura spit her drink in shock. It shot out of her mouth like a sprinkler across the table. My hand slammed over my mouth, and then I started laughing harder and harder. "Oh, my god! I don't know where that came from!" I kept laughing, and Xander snickered in my ear.

"Somewhere deep inside, babe."

"Careful, sweetheart," Crank muttered, as Xander passed the joint back to me. "It's laced with MDMA." My eyes widened.

"Seriously?" He nodded, and I laughed again. "You put ecstasy in your weed? Who are you smoking joints with?" I asked, and he grinned.

"Don't worry. My junk stopped working years ago. It's relaxing." I nodded and reclined back against Xander, as I took another toke off the joint. "Looks like you're going to be having some fun tonight, Gunner." Xander chuckled softly, as I passed the joint back to Crank.

"Depends on how she's feeling when everyone goes home," he joked, and I held his arms around me. I was starting to quickly relax in his arms. Almost to a drowsy state.

"It is relaxing. I've never done ecstasy before," I admitted and felt Xander's soft lips caress my forehead.

"You've never done ecstasy?" I slowly shook my head.

"My dad barely let me around pot," I admitted, and I felt myself jolt awake a few minutes later. The strangest feeling filled my body. I was relaxed, yes, but it was something else. Something... more. I ran my hands up Xander's forearm and a moan slipped through my lips. God, his skin felt so good. The soft hairs on his arm tickled my arm in the most pleasurable way.

"Are you alright, babe?" Xander whispered, and the sound of his voice had my clit tingling.

"Gunner, the MDMA hit her." Crank looked close at my face. "Yup, she's rolling, boss." I snorted as I played with Xander's arm hair between my fingers.

"Is that what this feeling is?" I rasped, and Xander softly chuckled in my ear. I turned my head and pressed my mouth to his, tangling my fingers through his hair, holding his mouth flush to mine. His tongue met mine in a dance of shattered wills and communicated my desires to him. Hell, right then, both of my deceased parents could've been standing there watching me make out with a man eighteen years older than me, and I would've kept doing it. A whimper and a moan slipped from my lips, as Xander teased the hem of my dress. It was black, sleeveless, paired with my dad's crew jacket.

"And that is our cue to exit," Trip said, and Danica laughed as they left.

I turned around in Xander's lap and straddled his waist. I went back to kissing him as he pushed my jacket down my shoulders.

"Fuck," he growled into my mouth, and I rubbed myself against him through our clothes. I needed him. I had to have him. I didn't care who saw or knew I was fucking him. His mouth traveled across my jaw and down my neck.

I rubbed my hand against his erection through his jeans that seemed to get smaller, as he hardened. I squeezed his stem repeatedly as he groaned.

"Xan," I breathed to him. "I need you to fuck me right now. Like, now, now."

He groaned and grabbed my ass through my dress.

"Leave the table, now," he demanded to the others, and they jumped up quickly. "Fuck, right here? There are a bunch of people around." I whimpered as he licked at the bowl at the base of my neck.

"I don't care. I need your cock in my pussy. I can't take it for another second." I started undoing his jeans, and he let out a husky moan.

"They'll know we're fucking, babe." Luckily, we were at a corner table, tucked away, but everyone would be able to see us and guess what was happening. I didn't give a shit.

"Oh, god… Xander… I'm so fucking horny." He pushed my panties to the side, and his cock slid home inside me. "Oh, yes." I rode him hard, as he reclined back in his seat, watching me work at him, and he stared at me, jaw slacked, desire caked in his honey-hazel eyes. "Xan, yes, yes, yes," I whispered over and over like a mantra, and his strong hands squeezed my ass.

"You're so fucking beautiful." He kissed me and massaged my breasts through my top. I groaned from my sensitive skin. Every touch, every caress, every thrust felt so different from normal, heightened. I was up in the clouds but quickly came down from the high's emotional part in just a moment.

Someone said something, I think. I couldn't really be sure. I was so focused on Xander, pleasuring him, and feeling him pleasuring me. I watched his face snap toward his crew, and he suddenly pushed me off of him out of nowhere. It left me whip lashed and confused.

"Wha…" He had his dick back in his pants and was stalking away from me before I had a chance to really react.

Hurt, confusion, and rejection filled me, as I stared after him. My flesh still buzzed, but the emotional high had been erased, replaced with a low. One I had never felt before. One I hoped I would never have to feel.

I moved off the table, rushed out of the bar, into the back, and barricaded myself in Derek's office. I curled onto the couch in the office and saw on the monitors that Xander was still talking to his crew.

He had abandoned being with me to talk to them. Tears cascaded down my face, as I cradled my face in my hands. I sobbed and cried and detested myself.

This was my fault. I had put myself up for this. I had sworn to myself long ago that I would never make my mom's mistakes, that I would never become her, but in my determination to avoid it, I had done exactly that. I had given a man that I barely knew my heart, and he had ripped it out easier and quicker than I expected.

My heart lay bleeding on the floor from Xander's rejection, and I was... broken.

Chapter 9

Xander

I was worried. No, fuck that. Worried didn't cover it. I was out of my damn mind. This was something that I wasn't comfortable with, wasn't used to.

I didn't get all bent out of shape about a woman, but here I was, drinking myself into a stupor because Jennifer fucking Saunders was ghosting me. She had been for seven fucking days. Since that night at the bar, Jen had been ignoring my existence. She disappeared suddenly after we had the most amazing sex of my fucking life when I had to deal with the disrespectful shit that was my newest member, Drill. All he had to do was say one thing, and I wanted to put a bullet between his eyes.

Save a piece for us. Some of us would like to take that dick-hopper for a drive, boss.

I was pissed, livid, way madder than I had ever been in my life. Jen was my woman, no one else. She sure as hell wasn't a dick hopper, and I would be damned if I ever let her be. It was a big rule of mine. No girl that I had ever dated was allowed to pledge to the crew. I was a bit of a selfish prick like that.

I gave Drill a piece of my mind. I threatened his life and drove the matter home for everyone that Jen was mine, my girl, and no one better even so much as look at her lustfully, or they would be answered to my nine.

When I had dealt with Drill, I saw that Jen was gone, disappeared. I knew she wasn't really gone because Liam's car was still outside, but I couldn't find her anywhere. I tried texting her to get her to come back out to me, but she didn't answer. That was a first. She had answered my texts before.

She had told me about her parents, why she had been fighting being with a biker so hard, and I got it. I understood where she was coming from. Trapper was a legend through the Black Stallions chapters, but obviously, he was a shitty husband and father. Hell, he drove his fucking wife to kill herself and didn't bat an eyelash. Who does that shit?

I wanted to be the guy she was with for years before she looked back and said to herself I'm glad I took a shot on him. I wanted to make Jen happy, and I thought she was... until she started ignoring me.

Fuck. I couldn't stop myself from sending her another drunk text. Was I losing my mind? Yeah, probably.

Xander: Jen, what's going on? You've been ghosting me for a week, and you disappeared that night at Derek's. Are you mad at me or something?

I didn't expect a response. I hadn't gotten one from the hundreds of texts I had sent over the past seven days. Why would this one be different? But, it was different. She did text me back, and I felt like some twelve-year-old geek who got his first erection from hearing the ding of my ringer.

Get. A. Grip.

I snatched my phone and opened the text, but my heart broke a bit right there.

Jen: Not mad, no. Leave me alone, Gunner. It's what you're good at.

It's what you're good at? That sunk a pit into my stomach. What? What was I good at? Leaving her alone? Fuck that. I sucked at that. The drunken texts should've proved that.

Fuck. Did Jen just dump my ass? I looked at the text again and nodded. Yup, she dumped me.

I had to decipher that. Leave me alone. It's what you're good at.

What the fuck did that really mean? What was she talking about? Me leaving her alone?

Suddenly, it hit me. I walked away from her to deal with Drill and, when I looked back at the table where she should've been, she was gone.

She was gone. She knew why I had to leave her like that, right? She had to have heard what Drill said or didn't she? Fuck, what if she hadn't?

She didn't. That was the problem, right? Shit. Did she think I had rejected her? Pushed her away to talk to my crew?

Shit. Shit. Shit.

How badly had I really fucked up with her?

* * *

I strolled into the bar by myself at ten that night. I had warned others to stay away.

I looked over to the bar and there was Jen. She was wearing a black apron, drying some glasses with a towel. She had the saddest expression on her face as she slowly rubbed the rag on the glasses. My heart broke a bit more at seeing her like that.

"Knock, knock," I muttered, and her eyes slowly lifted to mine before they narrowed. She set down the glass and the towel. She didn't speak, just stared at me. It was almost like she thought if she looked at me long enough that I would disappear. "Hey." I strolled over to the bar, and she still didn't speak. "Is Derek gone already?" She huffed at me.

"What do you want?" she asked, irritation across her face.

"We need to talk, Jen." She pulled off her apron and slammed it onto the counter.

"There's nothing to talk about. If you didn't come here for a drink, Gunner, you can leave." Then, she charged off into the back.

I felt defeated. She wouldn't even give me a chance to fix things or to even explain myself. Was I just kidding myself?

Maybe this was the universe's way of shitting on me.

Hey, Xander. Here's the best thing you could hope for. Whoops, psyche!

Yup, sounded about right.

Chapter 10

Jen

I laid in bed staring up at the blank ceiling, bubbles of emotion rising in my throat. Xander showing up at the bar last night had made me raw. I couldn't handle seeing him after how he hurt me.

I expected that once the ecstasy wore off, I would feel fine, but the pain was still present, and it got worse from seeing him. It took every ounce of self-control I had left not to cry. It was a struggle.

My heart was aching.

I turned toward the clean, white wall and spooned my pillow. Why couldn't he get the hint that he couldn't fix this? Why did he even want to? Was sex that important to him?

I wasn't important to him, or he wouldn't have walked out on me like he did that night.

I couldn't stop it. The tears fell. At first, it was one, but then another trailed the first. Soon, they were pouring down my face at an alarming rate, and it felt like my heart was being torn out of my chest.

The ache was too great. I couldn't stop it from consuming me.

Is this really just a broken heart? It felt way worse than I ever expected it to.

I had a flashback of being in bed with Xander, his fingers running through my hair as I kissed his chest. It was a simple memory, one with erotic undertones, but it was too much.

My tears turned into full-on sobbing.

"Jennifer!" Liam called for me, but I couldn't stop crying. "You have a visitor!" I didn't respond. I willed the tears to stop, but it didn't. The pain was too great.

It felt like forever, but it was only a couple of minutes before my sobs dried. I took a few breaths to calm down before I pulled myself out of bed.

My room had been pretty bare since I moved in, just a brand-new cherry oak dresser, a matching bedside table, and the full-sized bed that I was on, but now it felt so dark and gloomy. It was like everything was black, all color fading from the world. Even the sun seemed dark in my depression.

"I'll be down in a minute!" I croaked, dryly, before going to my adjoined bathroom. I threw some cool water on my face and tried to erase the puffiness of my eyes, but no amount of water could wash it away. I settled for makeup as my saving grace. I put on just enough to cover up how swollen my eyes were and how red my nose was. I looked presentable even if my eyes did look rather dead to me. Even the ocean blue color of my irises seemed dull and boring.

I put in some eye drops to clear up how red my eyes were before I emerged from the room. I strolled downstairs and was surprised to see Liam was gone, his car was gone, and Xander was standing before me.

Gone was his biker gear. In its place, Xander was wearing a nice navy blue button-down and some faded jeans. He had traded his biker boots for some tennis shoes. His short beard was gone, and his hair was combed.

This was very different from the Xander I had become used to seeing. He looked... presentable... which was unnerving. It shook my guard. It didn't bring it down, but it made it harder to keep up.

"Xander? Where is Liam?" I asked, nervously, and he gave me a kind smile. It wasn't his normal sexy smile. It was kind and sweet.

"He left. He was heading out of town." I looked around suspiciously. Was there some booby trap set up nearby? Was this a trap itself?

"What are you doing here?" He slowly and carefully walked over to me before softly taking his hands in mine.

"I came to apologize, Jen." I was stunned by this. Xander wanted to say he was sorry? For what? Was it his asshole behavior at the bar a week ago?

"For what?" I asked and eased my hands out of his. I crossed my arms over my chest, and his eyes narrowed.

"We both know, babe. I know I came off as being a raging dick a week ago at the bar. I didn't mean to. I swear. I wasn't trying to upset you or make you feel rejected. I should've realized you would be upset. I just figured you heard what Drill said and understood why I had to deal with him right then." Okay, now, I was confused.

"Um, deal with him?" The part of me that was protective of myself urged me to kick him out the door and refuse to see him ever again, quit my job, and leave California forever. The thing that stopped me was that I knew I needed to hear him out. He had brought down my defenses by showing up at my place of residence, dressed to impress.

"He said some majorly disrespectful stuff directed at you, and I wasn't going to stand for that. The worst bit was that he was saying it to me. I wasn't going to let something like that fly. He's new, which is probably the only reason I didn't kill him, to be honest. I wanted to. I really wanted to. I was so pissed that I was seeing red." Wow. Xander didn't ditch me to hang out with his crew? Drill had been bad-mouthing me?

"What did he say?" I asked, and a dark shadow fell across his eyes.

"Save a piece for us. Some of us would like to take that dick-hopper for a drive," Xander uttered with anger in his voice. Possessiveness radiated from his aura and jealousy encased his honey-hazel irises. The coloring in his eyes nearly disappeared, replaced with a near blackness that I had never seen before.

Xander hated Drill for wanting to put his hands on me.

"He said that? I'm surprised he's still alive. I can't say I'm surprised he said that considering he is the one who demanded I give him head in front of your crew when I went to the bar with Bruce." His eyes went wide before narrowing into menacing slits. Why is it that seeing Xander so pissed made my pussy so fucking wet? Was there something wrong with me?

Of course, Xander wasn't mad at me. He was mad at Drill, but still, Xander's hatred fueled my hormones in a way I didn't foresee.

"Fuck. He said that to you?" I slowly nodded.

"I didn't drop him the way I did just for calling me a doll." I tried to soften the blow a bit, but he was still pissed.

"Shit," he groaned, then moved closer to me. His mouth found mine possessively, and I clung to him, pulling him closer to me.

"Xan," he growled into my mouth and grabbed my ass through my Pokemon pajama pants, pulling my body against his. I moaned and whimpered as his tongue dug past my lips. I loved the feel of his barbell in my mouth and his hands gliding to my waist.

"Fuck," he grunted as he pulled out of the kiss. "Sorry. I'm not trying to—" I didn't give him a chance to finish that statement. I knew what he was trying to say, but it wasn't necessary.

"It's okay, Xan." I gave him a soft kiss on his chin, then his masculine jawline. "I miss the beard," I teased him, and he laughed.

"I figured you would be into the clean shave." I snickered before rolling my eyes.

"Other than using it to tickle me, I like the beard. I like the shave, but it makes you look really young. A bit unsettling, really. You're hot no matter what you do with your facial hair." I gave him a sexy smirk, and he returned it.

"Really?" I hummed, then kissed him again. "So are we okay?" he asked, sounding oddly like a five-year-old child that had screwed up.

"More than okay. You know, it's a big turn on when you're all pissed and jealous." He gave me that flirtatious smirk and winked at me.

"We're going to need to do something about that." He grabbed my ass in my unflattering Pokemon pajama pants, and I moaned before kissing him.

* * *

I walked Xander out to his motorcycle when a big, yellow moving truck drove up and parked, blocking the driveway. I was appalled, and Xander just laughed.

"Seriously?" I groaned.

"Calm down. We'll just talk to the driver." Xander tried to calm me down, but nothing pissed me off more than an obnoxious, self-centered motorist.

"Oh, I'm going to do more than just talk," I said to Xander as I walked over to the truck. "Hey, fucknut! What do you think you're doing?!" I slapped the side of the truck. I wasn't expecting the driver to walk around the side behind me.

"Fucknut? Is that any way to greet an old friend, Jennifer?" I spun around, recognizing the feminine voice, and screamed before slamming a hand over my heart. The eyes of my childhood best friend widened, and she laughed.

"Holy shit! Meg?" I smiled big, and she hugged me. "Fuck, you're in America?"

"Yes, I am. Crazy, right? Well, what did you expect, dearie? You run off out of nowhere and don't even make a pit stop at home to say goodbye to your best friend. If I didn't deduct that you were in trouble, I might be stark raving mad, love. Let me guess, that bastard of an uncle?" I shrugged before grinning.

"An even bigger bastard now. That is neither here nor there. How in bloody hell are you here? I haven't forgotten that you're... ." I trailed off, unsure if I should say it in front of Xander.

"Club property? Yeah, no shit, dearie. You obviously haven't heard yet." I was perplexed.

"Heard? Heard what?"

"There is rebelling within the organization. Those loyal to you and your father are trying to split off from your uncle. The Sergeant in Arms is leading the rebellion as of now. There are some demanding retaliation against Crack for his crimes against Trapper and you. There are a lot of the Black Stallions siding with you, ready to be led by you." I felt like the air had completely left my body in an instant. My brain was foggy, and I felt uneasy on my feet. Her news had rocked me to my core.

"What? That's impossible, Meg."

"It's true, Jen."

"No, it's not. Even if it was, which it isn't, I don't want it. I never did, and my father wouldn't listen to me. Crack wouldn't listen either," I explained, and she huffed.

"That's not the point, Jen. Crack crossed a line, and everyone sees it. He's a fucking prick that has no business in leadership. He turned his own brother into bread loaves not to mention Skater as well." Bread loaves were slang for killing someone, and my heart nearly stopped from what Meg had said.

"Wait, Skater? Why?" Meg frowned.

"He called Crack an 'incestual rapist fucknut', and openly said that you should lead the club because you've seen every aspect of it. You were one of the boys and one of the girls. He preached about you needing to start a revolution in the chapter, and Crack put him down. After that, everyone started jumping on the Team Jen train." I was pretty dumbfounded. Skater was a sweetheart, and he cared about everyone. He would've made a great president for the club.

"Well, fuck."

"Enough of the heavy. I brought a surprise for you." Meg squealed, and I was still in a daze from what she had told me. I had completely forgotten that Xander was still standing there. "Oh, hi!" Meg stopped and waved at Xander. I frowned at him and looked between them curiously. "Is that Liam?" she whispered to me, and I quickly shook my head.

"Make sure he doesn't hear you say that. It might offend the great and terrible Gunner," I teased in her ear, and she looked at me perplexed.

"Um, who?" I rolled my eyes and nodded Xander over before taking his hand in mine.

"Xan, this is Meghan Harper, one of my good friends from Sydney." He nodded with a soft smile on his face. "Meg, this is Alexander Davenport, A.K.A. Gunner, A.K.A. the president of the Black Stallions chapter in San Jose, A.K.A. my boyfriend." Okay, that one word was so fucking weird to say. I had never actually called someone my boyfriend. No one except Xander. His grin doubled in size, and Meg's eyes widened.

"Wait, there are Black Stallions out here?" I nodded.

"Meg, you're club property. How do you not know that?"

"Girl, I don't pay attention to that shit, not that it would make much of a difference anyway. Not every female in the organization back in Sydney could ride with the boys like Doll." She practically slurred my club name, and I scowled. I hated that name.

"Doll?" Xander asked as he threw his arm around my shoulder.

"Oh, he doesn't know?" Meg asked, surprised. "Jen is the only patched female member back in Sydney. Everyone called her Doll, and she hated it. Everyone treated her like a porcelain doll, which is where the nickname came from. She was one of the boys, and yet still one of the girls. Fucking sexist pigs."

"Speaking of sexist pigs, who the hell let you leave?" She shrugged nonchalantly.

"You left."

"I was running for my life. You obviously aren't," I rebutted, and she snickered.

"Babe, everyone left. The untouchables, house mouses, den mothers, and property. Poof," she stated, and my jaw dropped.

"Seriously? Well, shit."

"Yeah, call it a revolt. One night, all of us just disappeared." My eyes widened. "We took a stand in the name of Jen Saunders. We were all done with the bullshit. They were your family, and they did what they did to you? You know, Crack recorded that shit?" I gulped from what she said, and I felt the color drain from my face.

"What?"

"Yeah. Flashed it around at a meeting as a warning. 'This is what happens if you defy me,'" she explained, and my body stiffened.

"What is she talking about?" Xander spoke up, and I bit my lip nervously. I didn't get nervous, but I never wanted Xander to find out what happened.

"Um, I'll give you a minute." Meg took a step back and went around the truck, as I turned to Xander, worry across his face.

"Jen, what's the matter?" He gently touched my face, and it melted away all of my stress. I leaned into him, feeling like everything was right in the world as long as he touched me.

"I left out a part of the story about what happened with Crack." He slowly nodded, and I wrapped my arms around his waist. My arms were shaking, and his eyes narrowed with sadness.

"Baby, what did he do to you?"

"It's not what he did. It's what he tried to do." He nodded for me to continue. "My dad was very protective of me. He didn't even want guys to look in my general direction, and Crank was mad when my dad picked me to be his successor, so he wanted to turn me into a mouse," I explained, and he sighed.

"Okay?"

"He and a bunch of his guys jumped me and tried to… rape me. I fought my way out, and that's the end of it." His expression was blank, and I was worried until he pressed a soft kiss to my forehead, pulling me into his arms.

"God, Jen. Why didn't you tell me before?" Tears collected in my eyes as I clung to him with everything in me.

"I wanted to forget," I whispered brokenly, and Xander just held me tight for a while. It was exactly what I needed.

Chapter 11

Xander

Things with Jen had been fucking incredible. We had been together six months now. The sex was out of this world, and we couldn't get enough of each other.

No matter how amazing it was though, I couldn't escape the thought of when she might get tired of me. Did she really care about me, or was all of this just fun to her? I had no fucking clue but hey, the sex was good while it lasted. Carpe diem, right?

There were times when we would be together, and I was in sheer bliss with her, and other times my mind just wouldn't stop running. It was nauseating how messed up I was about this.

Maybe if she said she loved me, I could calm down and just be happy to be with her instead of waiting for the other shoe to drop. Maybe, I was just fucking cursed.

I had fucked a lot of girls but dating them? That couldn't have been more than I could count on one hand, and they all ended tragically. Too bad that Jen and I might be fated to go the same way.

CHAPTER 11

* * *

I was at the private clubhouse. It was a house in a nice neighborhood of San Jose where Crank and a few of the house mouses resided. It was also where my office was, so I spent a lot of time there.

"Hey, Gunner!" Meg waved at me as she walked by. Turns out some girls just plain like being whores. Jen's best friend left the chapter in Sydney just to pledge herself to our chapter. I figured she wanted out but no, she jumped right back in, and she was a favorite for the guys into accents and blondes. Bolt and Chain sure took a liking to her quickly. That woman was pretty much down for anything.

One night, a few months ago, she laid herself out naked on the kitchen table and had a full train run on her. A lot of the guys were into it and so was Meg. Screaming and moaning and begging someone to please shove a cock down her throat. Not that I was paying close attention to it or anything...

Okay, fine, yeah. I watched the whole fucking thing, and my dick throbbed watching her perform. I hadn't seen action like that in the club fucking ever, and I wanted to jump in and shove my dick down her throat, but I didn't. I stood at the door of my office and watched as a good number of my brothers fucked the shit out of her like some pussy-whipped asshole while she watched... me.

Meg was Jen's best friend, but no one could deny that she wanted me. It was obvious the first day I met her. Her eyes just kept falling to my dick, but she never made a move.

So yeah, we eye fucked the shit out of each other while she got screwed by thirty-two different guys. She only said anything to me once.

"Clear it with Jen, and you can join in, Gunner." That filthy tongue of hers moaned at me, and it took all of my self-control not to walk over and shove my cock straight down her throat.

Ever since that day, my balls have been in a vice whenever Meg is around. I see her, and I remember that night, her beckoning me with her tongue, showing me how wide her mouth could go, her on the decrepit table. If I was remembering correctly, that was the night that table finally broke in half.

Fuck.

"Oh, Xan?" Meg poked her head in again, and I snapped my head up, glad that my erection was successfully concealed.

"Yeah, sweetheart?" I muttered, and she grinned.

"Jen wanted me to let you know about dinner tonight, Liam's place, eight o'clock. Don't be late!" She squealed before bouncing out of the room, and I watched her leave, baffled by the fangirling, teenybopper like behavior.

Okay, that was odd. What was up with her? If I could chance walking around without my dick springing, I would ask, but I wasn't going to rock the boat. She might ask to service me, and I might actually give in.

* * *

I was running late. I got to Liam's house at eight-thirty, and Liam was walking out the door.

96

CHAPTER 11

"The place is all yours. Good luck." He laughed before jogging past me. Jesus fucking Christ. Everyone was acting weird.

I pushed open the door to hear laughter coming from the kitchen.

"Jen?" I called out.

"In here!" I walked through the living room, past the stairs, and into the expansive kitchen. I was surprised to see Meg was there with Jen, and they were laughing while undoing the to-go container from a Chinese restaurant.

"What's going on?" I asked, and Jen smirked at me.

"Hey, Xan. You're late." She walked over to me and gave me a big, sloppy kiss. If she didn't stop that, I would bust a nut. I was already hard from seeing Meg there.

"Sorry, babe." She grinned.

"Come on. I'm starving. I hope you don't mind that Meg is joining us." I shook my head quickly.

"No, not at all." Not as long as you don't catch me staring at her lips, thinking of them sucking my cock. I didn't mind a fucking bit.

"Awesome!" The girls brought the containers over to the table, and Jen handed me the plates before all three of us sat at the table. Jen sat across from me but next to Meg who seemed to be glancing between us a lot like she was waiting for something.

All of us made our plates, and Meg was idly chatting with Jen as she nodded along, laughing appropriately. I was getting antsy. Something was happening

97

here. I just wasn't sure what.

I stayed silent, watching the two of them. I noticed Meg started touching Jen's leg, but it was an innocent touch. Not flirtatious or overly friendly. It was more of a show that she was paying close attention.

It got to the point where we all finished eating, and the girls were each drinking a glass of Jack, still talking.

"Okay, so what's this all about?" I asked, curiously, and Jen's eyes widened.

"Oh, that's right. I completely forgot," Jen said, and Meg laughed.

"It's alright. I completely blanked it from my mind, and earlier, I had a hard time keeping my mouth shut," Meg stated, and Jen smirked.

"But you did right? You didn't tell him?" Meg threw her hand across her breast which was practically falling out of her mini dress. I could almost see her fucking nipple at the dip of her dress.

"I swear on my right tit. If he figured out anything, it was from my giddiness," Meg said before sipping her drink.

"Okay, what is going on? You two look chummier than normal." Jen laughed.

"Well, we were talking this morning, and Meg told me quite the story of a party a couple of months ago where she had a train run on her." Fuck. Just… fuck.

"It was amazing. Even the other girls seemed to enjoy the show. Even Danica was cheering me on, and she is about as prudish as a den mother can get, babe," Meg added, and Jen nodded.

"And she told me about how the entire time you were watching like you wanted to devour her." Jesus fucking Christ. It's official. Jen was about to dump my ass.

"Fuck, Meg. What happens in the clubhouse stays in the clubhouse, remember?" I grumbled, in irritation.

"Oh, please, Xander! She's my best friend, and it's not like she's mad." My eyes widened in surprise as Meg laughed. "Plus, I did tell you to call her for permission to join. You didn't."

"Wait, you're not mad?" Jen just smirked at me.

"Nope. Not at all. Do you really not know me at all by now, Xan?" She had a teasing tone to her voice, as she sipped her drink.

"Okay, so what is this about?" Jen grinned, and so did Meg.

"That reminds me. Did you know that Jen and I used to... fuck?" Meg asked, and I think I went into full-on shock.

"Excuse me?" Jen nodded.

"Yup. My first time was with Meg and... shit, what was his name again?" Jen asked, and Meg cackled.

"James. James Schmidt. He was a Bred-In. He was so nervous. He was shaking. You would've thought it was his first time," Meg explained zealously, and Jen snorted.

"I think it was his first time."

"No, it wasn't."

"How would you know?" Jen asked, surprised.

"Because I was his first time, a year before." Jen's eyes widened, and Meg nodded. "Yeah, you remember his dad, Buddy?" Jen nodded.

"Yeah, big old teddy bear. He was the Sergeant in Arms before he left the club."

"Well, he came to me and asked me to fuck James when the kid was seventeen." Wait, what? Was this girl serious?

"Holy shit! Seriously? That was against the rules then. Club property couldn't fuck anyone outside of the club."

"I know, but poor Buddy was desperate. He knew his son would never lose his virginity without some help. I felt bad for the kid and, plus, I love sex, so I fucked him. Trapper wasn't even pissed that Buddy asked me to do it because it was James. He was scrawny and shy and the kid had zero chances with girls." Jen rolled her eyes.

"Holy shit. I'm embarrassed to say I fucked that boy. He's even more pitiful than I thought." Meg laughed, and I rolled my eyes. I didn't want to hear about Jen's or Meg's sex life at all. Jen was my girlfriend. We had been together for six months, longer than any relationship I had ever had. Meg, on the other hand, was my forbidden fruit.

"Back to what this is about?" I asked, and the girls laughed.

"Sorry," Meg said, sheepishly. "Anyway, so we used to fuck like all the fucking time. As I've said, I love sex, and Jen never saw herself being the romantic, mushy girlfriend type. Whenever one of us was horny, we would call each other and fuck." Jen nodded along with Meg. "I swear, the things this woman could do with her tongue." Meg let out a shiver mixed with a dramatic moan.

"Bitch, some lesbo died the moment you decided you preferred dicks to clits." Jen grinned.

"Aw! Thanks." Meg moaned again. Stop fucking moaning. My dick was already hurting before she started doing that.

"Just remembering it is getting me all horny," Meg admitted, and I adjusted my jeans so my dick wasn't pressed against my zipper.

"Anyway, knowing that bit of a back story, we were talking, and we came up with an idea. I know you haven't fucked Meg, and I appreciate that considering that it's obvious that you want to fuck Meg." Fucking Meg grinned like the Cheshire Cat. "We wanted to see if you would be interested in… a ménage à trois with me and Meg." I think I went into complete shock. A fucking three-way?

"I'm sorry. I don't think I heard you right. I could've sworn you asked for a threesome," I grumbled while my dick pulsed, and Jen bit her lip.

"See, sex between me and Jen was always good," Meg stated.

"Great, actually," Jen inserted.

"But that threesome we had with James sucked a bunch. We always wanted to try again with someone more equipped for it than him, but we never found someone we both were attracted to who seemed to fit the bill… until now, and you obviously are attracted to both of us. Jen and I are comfortable enough with each other that there is never any jealousy between us." Jen nodded in agreement.

"Totally," Jen said, and I just stared at them.

"You are… serious?" My eyes fell on Jen who was smirking at me.

"Completely, right?" Meg stated, enthusiastically.

"It's all up to you, babe." Jen mused before the both of them stood up and sauntered over to me in their own catwalks, sexily sliding around the table to me. I sat back in my chair as they bent down in front of me, and Jen slowly worked on my belt while Meg rubbed my dick through my jeans.

"Oh, my god. His dick is big." Meg whispered in Jen's ear, and she nodded, popping my dick out of my pants. She stroked my shaft a few times, and I groaned as I watched Jen look at Meg.

"Go ahead." Meg grinned, then took my cock into her mouth. My jaw slacked in pleasure as Meg teased my ring and gagged herself on my length, whimpering and moaning.

"Fuck," I groaned as Jen took my hand, kissing my knuckles, before pressing my hand to Meg's head.

"Good girl. Keep sucking his dick. He loves it when you deep throat him." Meg nodded, and I held her head down, fucking her mouth.

"Fucking shit," I grunted, as Jen reached into my jeans and kneaded my balls, adding to the ecstasy. "Oh, my god... so fucking good," I moaned as I fucked Meg's face, and Jen stood up, still playing with my balls, and kissed me.

"She likes having her face fucked. The harder you do it, the wetter she gets. You want her nice and wet, don't you?" Jen whispered in my ear as she released my balls and walked behind me, rubbing my tense shoulders.

"You're really okay with this?" I asked as I dug my fingers in Meg's scalp and gave her it just a tad rougher. Her hand quickly yanked down my jeans to my ankles, and she covered her hand in her saliva from my base and started to tease my balls herself.

"Xan?" Jen whispered to me. "I want you to fuck both of us, and I want to watch you fuck her. I want her to watch you fuck me, and I want you to watch me and her fuck each other. Most of all, I want to watch you fuck her face until she is desperate for her pussy to be touched. I want you to make her work for it." Holy fucking shit.

It was official. I was the luckiest bastard alive.

I stood up from my chair and grabbed the edge of the table, fucking Meg's face good and rough. She was whimpering and moaning, playing with my balls.

"That's right. Take it good." Jen sat on the floor next to Meg, and I watched as Meg released my balls and shoved her hand up Jen's dress. Jen's eyes fell as she moaned. "Oh, shit. Slow it down, Meg," Jen whimpered, then Meg pulled her head back.

"Fuck, you taste so good." She gasped for air, and I grabbed her head.

"I never said you could stop. Get that dick back in your fucking mouth." Meg grinned and pumped my cock with her talented hand as Jen started sucking on my balls.

"As you wish," Meg moaned, then took me back in her mouth as both Meg and Jen worked me toward my release.

Chapter 12

Xander

Those girls loved on my dick so good at the kitchen table that I busted my nut in less than five minutes down Meg's throat. She whimpered and mewled as she clawed at my thighs. Fuck, she was incredible at taking a face fucking. Not all girls could handle it.

Jen dragged me up to her room with Meg in tow, and both girls stripped naked. I was about to climb into bed with them, but Jen stopped me. She made me sit in a fucking chair near the end of the bed.

"Enjoy the show," she teased me, and I relaxed in the chair as Jen and Meg started to kiss. Fuck, that was hot. I could see their tongues fighting for dominance, as they played with each other's nipples, and Meg ran her hands down Jen's torso to her delicious pussy. Jen started whimpering, and they pulled apart. Meg grinned, and Jen nodded, as she sat on the edge of the bed, legs spread wide. I watched as Meg bent over, her ass and pussy on full view for me, and spread Jen's pussy open. Then, Meg started to devour her. Jen's jaw slacked, as she mewled erotically. "Oh, fuck," she whimpered, and I could see from the way Meg's cheeks were flexing that she was surely doing some insane shit with her tongue.

"Shit, I missed eating your pussy. It's so fucking good, like the best fucking honey ever." Then, Meg went back to Jen's pussy as Jen moaned, pawing at her breast.

"Make my pussy feel good then. Oh, yes." Jen fell back against the bed, and Meg threw her legs over her shoulders, taking Jen's pussy exactly how she desired. I watched Meg's cheeks vibrate at a crazy pace as Jen gasped, whimpering, almost to tears. Well, shit. I could never get Jen to almost cry with pleasure. I was a bit envious, but I was way more turned on. "Oh, my fucking god. shit, don't stop. Faster, faster, faster!" Jen cried out, as she gripped hard on Meg's hair, holding her mouth against her pussy. "Holy fucking god, yes! Ugh, fucking shit! I'm going to come!" Meg nodded, then I watched in amazement, as Meg shoved a finger up Jen's ass, then another and another. Jen screamed in pleasure, and my dick sprung. Jen yelled repeatedly, as Meg kept at her pussy. Jen relaxed against the bed and whimpered. "Oh, my god. You made me come so good." Meg nodded as she kept at Jen's pussy.

"Let me keep going, please. I need to make you come more. I missed tasting this. I could cum from your delicious nectar. So fucking sweet." Then, Meg went back down, and Jen moaned as she let Meg eat her out again and again and fucking again. Meg was on a roll, making Jen scream into orgasm after fucking orgasm.

I wanted to join them, but I loved watching.

Jen turned her head and looked at me as she came down from her fifth orgasm by Meg's tongue, and I slowly rubbed my dick. She nodded to me as she moaned and whimpered.

That was my cue. She was telling me to join.

I stood and walked up behind Meg and sunk my cock hard into her sweet, dripping wet tightness. She came up for air, gasping loud, and I shoved her face back in Jen's pussy.

"Keep eating her out until I say so. Got it?" I whispered to Meg, and she nodded, as I spanked her ass, getting a whimper from her. "Give it to her good, or I take out my dick." Then, Meg really got back to how she had been devouring Jen. Jen started clawing at Meg's scalp as she cried out.

"Oh, my god. She's been doing so good. Give it to her deep, baby. She's earned it." I nodded vigorously, and she whimpered.

"Deep and hard, or deep and slow?" I asked Jen, and she moaned.

"Hard. Give her a good fucking." I nodded and tightened my grip on Meg's hips before I pounded her hard, fast, and deep. Meg whimpered and cried into Jen's pussy. I slammed my cock deep into her convulsing core, as Jen moaned. "How does it feel?" Jen suddenly asked me, and I grunted.

"Fucking good. So fucking tight. I don't think she's getting fucked enough." Then, I took a handful of Meg's hair, yanking her head away from Jen's pussy. Jen laid there spent as Meg moaned out for me.

"Ah! Ah, yeah, like that!" she whimpered as I spanked her ass hard. "That's right, Xan! Fuck me like you mean it." I growled, as Jen slipped down onto the floor in front of Meg and, from the loud moaning and screaming Meg gave, I assumed Jen was eating her clit while I fucked her. "Ah, ah, ah! Fuck!" Meg cried out as I forced her face into the mattress and pounded her like my only goal was getting off, but I wouldn't come anytime soon. The point was abusing the fuck out of her g-spot, make her delirious with desire. "Keep going, keep going! Don't stop!" Meg begged and turned her head to look at me as I ravished the shit out of her. Her eyes were hazy with need as she moaned. I don't know what came over me, but the next thing I knew I was kissing her juicy sweet lips.

I kept pounding away at her, and she held my mouth to hers as she whimpered and moaned. Meg orgasmed hard, clawing her nails at my hip, and after that,

Jen slipped away. I wasn't really paying attention with my dick deep in Meg.

I flipped Meg onto her back and climbed on her before slipping my cock back inside her.

"Fuck, so tight." I groaned before kissing her again. Mmmm, I could taste Jen's pussy on her lips. So fucking delicious.

"Shit, please, come," Meg begged as I fucked her hard.

"Are you getting tired of my dick already?" I asked, and she shook her head.

"It's so good. I'm not used to guys as big as you." I got what she meant. She was getting sore. She had gotten off a couple of times already, and Jen got a bunch of orgasms. Most of mine were mental which was fine.

"I can stop. You got me off pretty good in the kitchen." She gave me a thankful smile, as I pulled out of her. She let out a cute little kitten moan, and I flopped on the bed next to her.

"Fuck, that was incredible." She snickered, and I smirked.

"Thanks," I mumbled, as I caught my breath.

"Was that because of the piercing?" she asked, curiously, and I shrugged.

"About half that actually."

"Well, damn. I bet women cried everywhere when Jen locked your ass down."

"What is that supposed to mean? Locked me down?" She chortled.

"You know, because you're her man, and she's your girl. You guys are exclusive, and you seem really happy together." I frowned from what she said.

"Are you sure about that?" I asked, self-consciously.

"About what?" she inquired, and I sighed.

"That Jen's happy with me." She suddenly gasped before sitting up suddenly.

"You're kidding me, right?" I didn't respond, just stared at the ceiling. "God, Xander, of course, she is. Jen doesn't get attached to guys, but she's nuts about you. She talks about you all the time. Jen fucking loves you, man, and that's no small feat." Wait, what? I looked at Meg surprised and saw a smirk on her face.

"She said that? She loves me?" Meg snickered.

"All the fucking time. Trust me, if she didn't, she wouldn't still be with you. You two will probably end up being one of those club success stories. Get married, live happily ever after until, you know, you croak." I had to laugh at the end of her statement then smiled.

"Thanks, Meg. I appreciate that. It means a lot coming from Jen's best friend." She nodded then looked around.

"Hey, where did she go?"

"Maybe the bathroom?" I shrugged, then heard a scream from downstairs.

"LET ME GO! STOP IT! XANDER!" My heart raced from the panicked sound of Jen's voice. Instincts kicked in, and I grabbed my jeans, tearing them up my legs, running toward the stairs.

"Jen?!" I made it to the top of the stairs as I saw three guys I didn't recognize in

Black Stallions colors dragging her out of the house, kicking and screaming.

"Help me! Help, please!" she cried, and I propelled myself over the railing, tumbling to the ground. It was a high jump but faster than trying the stairs.

"Jen!" Next thing I knew, those men were tossing her in a black van and speeding off with her screaming in the back.

Adrenaline was racing in my veins, as I ran to the end of the driveway, no longer seeing the van. All I could see was trees and pavement.

"No, no, no," I groaned as I gripped my hair relentlessly in my hands, tugging on the roots.

"Xander, what happened?" Meg ran outside back in her dress as frustrated tears ran down my face.

"They grabbed her. They fucking took Jen." She gasped and scanned the street.

"It has to be Crack, but how? When I left, I took everything that could lead anyone to her with me. There is no way he could've found her unless someone ratted her out." I groaned aloud.

"It doesn't fucking matter! They took her. A bunch of guys wearing Black Stallions colors that I don't know broke into Liam's house while I was there, when I could've protected her, and took her." My voice broke as tears streamed down my face, and her expression crumbled.

"Xander..." I sobbed.

"She's fucking gone, Meg. I was supposed to protect her. Liam brought her to me to keep her safe, and I fucking failed. I didn't even know she loved me.

I never got to tell her how much I fucking loved her, how knowing she was there would keep me from slipping into fucking darkness. I never said it, and now I never can. Jen's gone, and they're going to kill her. She's probably already dead." Meg walked up to me and slapped me out of nowhere.

"Get your head together, Xander. It's not over yet, okay? She's alive. Crack wants to finish what he started, give her the punishment he thinks she deserves. That means, make her suffer, which takes time. Either Crack is already here, or he is on his way personally. This is not the time to be losing your shit, Xander. Got it?" Fuck, she sounded like me. She was right though. We had some time to save Jen, and that was what I planned to do.

Chapter 13

Jen

I couldn't really explain it, but in a way, it messed with me seeing Xander kissing Meg. He was my boyfriend and, even though I never told him, I loved him like crazy. I knew that I wanted to spend my life with Xander and, yes, I asked him to have a threesome with me and Meg, but I never thought I would feel self-conscious about seeing Xander kissing someone else, even if it was a part of the deal.

It was a threesome. It was sex. Kissing happened. Hell, I kissed Meg in front of Xander, and he didn't seem bothered.

It was just me, and I had no right to be upset, so I left the room.

I could hear the loud banging and moaning from downstairs. They were still going at it. They probably didn't even notice me leave, not that I expected them to.

This was all on me.

I wanted to do this with Xander and Meg. Meg and I always talked about trying a three-way again, and then she told me how Xander had been watching her. It seemed perfect. There was an equal attraction all around.

It was incredible, way better than the only other time we did that, and the whole time, Xander had Meg's face shoved in my pussy, he was looking at me with lust and desire sparkling in his eyes. It was almost like he was imagining Meg was also me.

A big part of me wanted to do it again, the three of us fucking, but a small part of me was nervous to see Xander kissing Meg again. Maybe I needed to explain to them my issue, and we could work it out together. Yeah, that sounded right.

The banging stopped, so I figured they finished. I strolled into the kitchen with heavy feet, worrying about talking to Xander and Meg about this. I always loved Liam's kitchen. Sparkling white tile floors, marble countertops, stainless steel appliances, and an incredible deep, single-sided sink. I would walk in there and sometimes I would hear my mom's voice in the back of my head saying how this was a real kitchen. God, I missed her. That was probably why the kitchen filled me with nostalgia. It reminded me of my mom.

I grabbed three glasses of water and turned to take them upstairs when a dark figure appeared, his hand grasping my throat. It squeezed tight around my windpipe, and my oxygen was cut off. My lungs were ablaze, and my head was fogging up, but I fought. I kicked and punched with all the strength I had.

I almost gave up in shock when my vision cleared, and I recognized the face of the person before me. It was James Schmidt, Buddy's son, the same guy I gave my virginity to. He was wearing Stallion colors, and he had bulked up since I had last seen him. A black bandanna covered his short light blonde hair, his brown eyes seemed aged, and he had some scruff on his face.

I fought harder, and he loosened his grip on my neck. I struggled to gasp as he put his pointer finger to his lips, shushing me.

"James?" I mouthed, and he nodded before leaning into my ear.

"It's not safe. You need to go. Crack is here. Quick, slip out the back door," he ordered, and I stared at him amazed.

"Here? How?"

"It doesn't matter. You need to go, or you're dead."

"But my boyfriend and Meg are upstairs. I can't leave them."

"They'll be fine. Just go," James pressed and disappeared around the corner. "I don't think she's here," he said, and I looked around frantically. Sure, I could slip out the back door, but they would hear it. The back door was incredibly loud. The front door was silent though. If I could sneak over there, I could get out undetected, and I could warn Xander.

"Let's check upstairs." I heard one of the men say, and I panicked. If they went upstairs, they would find Meg and Xander. Xander didn't have his gun. I knew it was in his jacket at the table. Plus, if they saw Meg, she would be dead. She was club property and left. I had to protect them at all costs.

I couldn't leave. If I could get to Xander's gun, I had a shot of saving them. I tip-toed over to the kitchen table, and I accidentally kicked the table leg.

There was no way they didn't hear that.

I heard running, and I raced around the table, shuffling around his pockets. I felt the cool metal of his gun and went to grab it when I was yanked back.

"There you are, sweetheart." Brick. I recognized that voice. He was one of Crack's right-hand men. Panic filled me.

"Let me go!" I screamed and kicked him but suddenly, I was punched in the gut. My muscles were on fire and my body was screaming to collapse. "Stop it!" Then, I saw Crack standing there, a smug look on his face.

"We've got you now, Jennifer," he sneered with delight, and I nearly vomited.

"XANDER!" I screamed at the top of my lungs, fighting against Brick's tight grip. Then, we heard the loud, heavy footsteps upstairs. "Run!" I started to scream, but Brick slammed his hand over my mouth.

"Crack, there are people upstairs. We don't know how many. We have to get out of here." James panicked, and Crack nodded.

"Take her to the van. We will deal with this whore at the warehouse." I fought hard against Brick, but he was called that for a reason. He was a bodybuilder, and his muscles were tough as bricks.

"Jen!" I heard Xander and looked up at the top of the stairs, as I was being dragged toward the door. I bit Brick as hard as I could, and he hissed before pulling his hand away.

"Help me! Help, please!" I screamed at Xander, and then he disappeared from my field of vision. I knew this was his worst nightmare come to life. He knew what would happen if Crack found me, and I was being dragged away by men in Black Stallions vests that Xander had no way of knowing. I'm sure he put the pieces together.

"We've got a big welcome home party ready for you, Jen. Everyone is eagerly waiting to see you." I screamed out loud, as Brick tossed me into the van. I looked up and saw Xander running toward me.

"Xander!" They slammed the door closed, darkness surrounding me, and I cried, "I love you!" I never got to tell him how I felt. I was too fucking scared that he would reject me, but now I would never get to.

The van was musty. It smelled like dander, sweat, and blood. I touched the soaked carpet under me and lifted my hand. It was blood. My eyes trailed along the floor, looking for the source of the carnage, and I found it.

"Domino?" The San Jose Treasurer was lying on the floor, broken and bleeding. I crawled over to him as the van bounced around the streets. He was breathing raggedly and his body was trembling. "Domino, oh, god." How did they find him? Was he how they found me?

"Jen," he wheezed as I squeezed his hand. Domino was a sweet guy. He was the kind of guy who could make everyone smile and laugh, and he was loyal to a fault. At least I thought he was. "I tried," Domino groaned as blood trickled past his lips.

"You tried what?" I asked worried.

"I saw them at the... bar... with Laura.... She betrayed us all... I tried to stop them from... finding you, but I... failed." He coughed painfully, and I soothingly stroked his hair. Laura? Of all people, she was the one who ratted me out? Why?

She was nuts about Liam and I knew her and Xander had history but I assumed it was all in the past. Did she think there was something?

"You didn't fail, Domino. You stayed loyal to me and Gunner. Loyalty, respect, and family is what being a Black Stallion is all about, and you are all of that and more. I'm proud of you, Domino." My voice started cracking. This whole situation reminded me of when my dad died and all I wanted to do was save Domino. "Just hold on, okay? Gunner will be coming for us, and we will get you all patched up. Save your energy, okay?" Domino slowly nodded, and I continued the soothing circles on his soft hair.

The clock was ticking on mine and Domino's life. I had maybe a few hours before I was dead like my mom, like my dad.

At least Xander and Meg were safe.

* * *

I was yanked from Brick's van and let out a scream, hoping someone might hear me. The place was deserted, but there was the smallest chance that someone could call for help and save my life.

"Shut up." Brick threw his hand over my mouth and tossed me on his shoulder. I kicked and screamed and fought the rope tied around my wrists.

I dug my teeth into Brick's hand, drawing blood, and he groaned loudly. Suddenly, he threw my body against the wall of a warehouse we arrived at. My arms and legs hurt worse than they ever had.

"Not so rough, Brick. I've got plans for her," Crack snickered evilly, and I whimpered from the ground. I couldn't move.

"Yes, boss." I looked over to Crack and growled.

"You're an asshole. I'm supposed to be your family," I stated and slowly turned onto my side. All of a sudden, twenty guys came out of the warehouse and blocked me in.

"Sorry, sweetheart. The club above all else. You understand, right?" He wasn't the slightest bit sorry. I could feel the arrogance radiating from him, and I

116

groaned.

"You're no longer a princess, Doll," Brick said with a grin on his face.

"So what's your plan for me? Huh? Rape me and beat me to death?"

"Well, yes and no. We need some information from you," Crack said as Brick grabbed me by my arms and dragged me into the warehouse. The door was left wide open like they thought they were untouchable for whatever they had planned for me.

Aged, wooden crates scattered around the cement floor, dust discoloring the ground. It was pretty bare.

"Recognize this, sweetheart?" I looked up and saw it, the wood workbench, dusty, dirty, evil. That was what they had me pinned to when they tried to gang-rape me.

I instantly knew the first step of their plan. They wanted to break me, destroy my spirit, but I wouldn't let them. The sooner I did that, the sooner I would be dead. The only fighting chance I had was to hang on and defy their desires.

"Yup. Are you planning to make an orgy out of this, Crack? I am so shocked," I huffed sarcastically, and I didn't fight. There was no point. Could I escape five men? Sure, no problem. Could I escape twenty-five Stallions? Fuck no. I knew that.

I had to wait it out and hope and pray that Xander would find me.

"Am I that predictable?"

"Definitely. Bring it on." I didn't show fear or anxiety. I could survive this. I was one tough motherfucker. They would not break me.

Brick pulled me over to the workbench and forced me to straddle it while he bound my hands together with rusty, old chains. Well, that was a new feature to this show.

"You updated it? I'm impressed. Did you learn from last time?" I asked, though I didn't care.

"Glad I could impress you." Crack grabbed my hair and yanked my head back. "Don't get confused. This isn't meant to be pleasurable, but we will make you like it and hate that you like it."

"Good." He looked at me surprised. "I spent most of my teenage years hanging out with Meg. Who doesn't love a good gang bang?" He looked pissed from that. Good. He needed to be pissed. If he was happy, I wasn't doing my job right.

They could rape me but I would not like it. I would hate it. His men wouldn't know that though. I would give out the same physical responses I would for any man I decided to fuck but on the inside, I would be crying, begging them to stop.

I felt someone rip my dress straight down the middle, leaving me as naked as the day I was born.

"You get the honors of going first, Brick." Crack's voice boomed, then he walked away. Another guy came up in front of me, someone I didn't recognize. He dropped his pants, stroking his hard dick.

"Bite it, and I'll put a bullet between your eyes, bitch." He grabbed my head and shoved his dick in my mouth.

I didn't bite him. I was smart. I knew the best way to live the longest in the situation was to perform well. I had to embrace my inner Meg.

Using my chained hands, I pumped his base while sucking him good. He groaned and stopped thrusting at my face.

"Holy fuck. That's a good slut," he said, and I didn't let myself be offended.

I expected to feel someone shove their dick inside me. That was the point of this, right? What shocked me was I felt someone's mouth on my pussy. A big part of me was disgusted, but I had to push that away. Whoever it was, probably Brick, had a talented tongue, and my clit was tingling.

I whimpered on the cock in my mouth as someone spanked my ass. I looked up at him, and his eyes were foggy.

"Take it in your throat," he demanded, and my pussy started clenching from the way my pussy was being licked. I moaned and groaned as I took that cock into my throat, gulping around him, continuously. "Damn it. Brick, can I fuck her now?" the guy asked, and the mouth left my pussy.

"I think she's enjoying my mouth, man. The boss left. We can do whatever we want with her. You know his orders. Make her orgasm relentlessly. I think she likes your dick anyway. What do you say, sweetheart?" Brick said, before going back to sucking and licking at my pussy. I whimpered, and the man in front of me pulled my mouth back.

This was wrong. I shouldn't like it and a huge part of me didn't, but I couldn't let myself show it.

"Mmm, so tasty, baby." Brick sucked up my orgasm before he moved away. I glanced behind me, and the man who had his dick in my mouth a minute before, got up behind me, stroking his dick. "Go ahead, kid. I'm a patient man." I saw Brick working on his belt as he walked around to my face.

I felt the guy enter me, and I cried out. Then Brick came in front of me and forced his cock in my mouth.

On the outside, I was begging and pleading and orgasming like crazy. On the inside, I was crying, hoping it would stop. To stop myself from crying, I pictured Xander. I saw him holding me to him while he kissed my forehead, rubbing his hand down my back. I was already missing him.

My body kept responding through all the men who jumped between my mouth and raping me.

Only two guys didn't join in. Crack and James. James watched the whole thing but I could tell from his face that he wanted to vomit from what they did to me.

Chapter 14

Xander

I called an urgent meeting with the whole organization. I needed backup for this. I was running out of time, and I needed to find Jen fast.

"My house was the old clubhouse. I checked to see if anyone had been there to try to use its location, and I got zilch," I stated, as I leaned against the table, staring at the map.

"They could have her stashed in a hotel until Crack gets here," Glock offered up. "There are a couple of cheap ones within a few miles of Liam's house. We should search them and send someone to hit the docks as well." I slowly nodded.

"I just got off the phone with a low level patched member," Meg stated, as she jogged into the room. "Crack received a tip three days ago that Jen was in San Jose and even provided the address of where she was staying. Xander, the tip came from here, from the San Jose Black Stallions clubhouse." I was seeing red as my eyes scanned around the room. One of my own people betrayed my trust and narced on Jen.

"What the fuck? Who was it?" I sneered, and Meg touched my arm.

"Xan, it wasn't one of the guys. My source says... it was a woman, club property." That pissed me off.

I did everything I could to protect the girls. Even when it came out that a bunch of my guys were ignoring my no-rape rule. I discharged twenty-five of my guys, and one of the women I was protecting went behind my back and ratted out Jen.

I stormed out of the meeting room and charged into the living room where all the women were gathered, even pregnant Danica. She was rubbing her stomach, as the guys charged behind me, probably to protect their women from my wrath.

I didn't care who she was or her reasoning. I would kill her with my bare hands.

"Who did it?" All the women looked at me surprised. "Which one of you did this? One of you called them here and told them where to find Jen. Who was it?" The girls were looking around frantically.

"What? You haven't found her yet?" Danica asked, anxiously, and Trip went to her.

"Calm down, darling. She'll be fine. We'll get her back." Danica curled into her husband's embrace. The two had gotten hitched just two months ago, they were expecting a baby, and Jen was one of Danica's best friends. Definitely wasn't her. She was genuinely upset.

"Wait, where's Laura?" Carrie stated, and I took note that Laura was missing.

Laura? No, it couldn't be. Laura wouldn't do this. No matter what was happening, I knew Laura wouldn't do something like this to Jen. Scratch out the history between me and Laura, Jen was her friend. Laura was more likely to fight for Jen than to bring death to her doorstep.

"Laura?!" I called out and got nothing. She wasn't there. All the females were looking around, calling her name angrily. "Find her."

"I can help with that." I looked at the front door and was shocked and appalled by who I saw at the door.

"Dowry, what the fuck do you want?" I sneered. He was known as Drill before he was kicked to the curb for his disrespectful nature. He looked like crap, like he hadn't slept in a week, or had a decent meal in just as long. He was wearing jeans, a ragged t-shirt, and a black hoodie. He slowly pulled his green baseball cap off before looking around the room.

"Shit, it's Drill," I heard a couple of the girls whispering to each other. Everyone knew I had every reason to kick him to the curb and no one ever expected to see him again.

"I know I screwed myself out of being a part of the Black Stallions, but I still see everyone here as family which is why I'm here. I know where Jen is. I saw her being dragged into a warehouse by the docks in Alviso. She's alive." I could relax a bit at the news, but the stress came back from what he said. "You're going to want to kill every last one of those motherfuckers, Gunner. The things I saw them doing. No woman deserves that, definitely not Jen."

I shook his hand and pulled him in for a hug, which I'm sure surprised him and everyone else since I was the one who kicked him out. I was grateful that he was where he was exactly when he was and had the loyalty to come to me with this information. He might as well have saved Jen's life himself.

"Thank you." He hugged me back before stepping back. "Still got your bike?" I asked, and he grinned big.

"Never leave home without it. I'll show you where she is." I nodded and let out a loud whistle.

"Lock and load! We're rolling out, boys." Then, the girls rushed forward.

"We're coming, too. Jen is one of us. We want to help," Carrie demanded, and I looked around at all the women looking at me like they were ready for battle.

"You ladies sure?" I asked, and they all nodded.

"Yes, no girl left behind." That was DeeDee and I rolled my eyes.

"Fine. We might need extra hands." The women cheered. "Everyone, get geared up!" Crank opened the safes full of guns and armed the women, while I grabbed my vest and made a quick stop at my office.

I grabbed Drill's old vest from my desk drawer and walked out as everyone was hopping on their bikes.

"Dowry?!" I called to him, and he came rushing over, looking ready for battle.

"Yeah, boss?"

"You're missing something." I handed him his colors, and his eyes widened in surprise.

"Wait, really?" I nodded, then smirked.

"Welcome back. It seems you finally learned what it means to be part of the Black Stallion. It's about family, loyalty, and respect. Even though you were discharged, you came to me and told me where Jen is. That's loyalty. That's what a family does." He grinned and nodded.

"I won't let you down."

"Welcome back, Drill." I patted his shoulder and made my way to my bike. "Drill, you lead the way."

"Aye aye, Captain!"

* * *

I was on edge as my club's full mass, other than Danica, rode through the winding roads. Trees whipped by like an infinite forest. Headlights zoomed in the opposite direction of us.

Adrenaline coursed through my veins, and my arteries were on fire with anticipation. I was heading into battle, and everyone knew it. Some of my crew could die and maybe that made me selfish, putting Jen above everyone else. Jen was the single most important person in my life, and I loved her.

This whole situation put so many things in perspective. Me and Jen. The club. My life. Our future.

I could still feel her hands on my face, feel her lips on mine, and smell her sweet honeysuckle scent. I would not lose her. No matter what, I wouldn't let Crack win.

I sped through the highway and took a side road that led to the docks. Drill started to slow down his bike, and everyone else slowed down too. Then, even over the loud rumble of the bikes, I heard it.

A loud, pained yell full of anguish and suffering. It was from Jen. I knew it.

I jumped off my bike and went running to her, but Drill grabbed me, stopping it.

"What are you doing? You can't just run in there half-cocked. There are a lot of guys in there." Drill held me in place. "If you run in there ahead of everyone, you'll get yourself killed, Xander." I groaned in frustration.

"They're hurting her in there. I can't do nothing." I yelled in frustration. I needed to save Jen.

"Don't worry. We just have to go in together, weapons drawn." Everyone pulled out their guns, and we approached the warehouse to hear another cry of pain from her.

I'm coming, Jen.

We made it to the door, and we walked in with our guns ready to kill.

"Back the fuck away!" I said, before I even saw the heartbreaking scene in there. Jen was naked, covered in bruises, cuts, and blood. There was so much blood. Her lip was busted, and she looked like she had zero strength left. Blood was running down her face from a cut across her forehead. She was heaving for breath.

I caught the heartbreaking sight of a trail of dried blood between her legs that was older than the rest, and I knew she wasn't on her period.

Those fuckheads raped her. Drill was right. They all deserved to die for what happened here.

Ropes tied Jen down to a wood-framed chair. She probably could've escaped it when she was first tied down if she tried, but she wouldn't be able to get away from the twenty plus guys surrounding her.

"The legendary San Jose Black Stallions!" A man stood beside Jen, clapping his hands. "I was wondering when you would show up. Some of my new friends thought you would be a lot quicker than that. Xander, isn't it?" Jen lifted her eyes, and they met mine.

"Help. . . her," she mumbled, and my heart broke. Her? Who was she talking about?

"My men call me Gunner, and you're attacking my woman." The man beside her held an aluminum baseball bat, tapping it against the leg of her chair. That bat was covered in thick flesh and blood. My eyes drifted to his feet from the blood trickling off the bat and caught the sight of Laura's mangled body. She looked dead.

Laura, the sweetest, nicest club girl I had ever known, was beaten, almost unrecognizable. Her blonde hair matted with blood, the red stains going down the length of her white dress, and over her stomach, swollen with her unborn child. The sight of her made me want to break down. She was a woman that I had loved and cared for the duration of sixteen years. I wanted to protect her and yet I couldn't. She was gone.

"He killed her," Jen mumbled as my eyes snapped back up to her. "She tried to help, and he... he killed her. She was... naive... she didn't realize what he had planned for me. Isn't that right, Uncle?" Jen mumbled then Crack patted her head, completely ignoring her.

Laura was the one who brought them here? She wasn't a naive girl. What had she been thinking? I never would've believed it if Jen hadn't said it. Laura wouldn't have betrayed me so why did this happen?

Crack directed his statement at me, "I recognize you from the house earlier. You seemed rather attached to her." Then, he patted her head again. "You see, my niece, sweet Jennifer, has been holding back information from me, and I intend to get it out of her, so scurry along back to your cozy lives." He gestured for us to leave, and I cocked my gun. Was this fucker serious? Even if Jen wasn't my girlfriend, just address me and my men like that, would get him killed. Plus, the bastard had murdered Laura. He needed to die.

"Not happening." The rest of my small army came inside, guns drawn, waiting for the chance to strike. "Jen is mine. This is my fucking territory, and I'm not leaving without her. Hand her over or everyone dies tonight." Crack made an amused yet displeased face and made a repetitive tsk noise while shaking his head.

He had some major fucking balls. I outnumbered him by over three times as many people.

"Sure, why not? I'll just remove this." He grabbed a knife that was sticking out of Jen's leg and yanked it out. She groaned dramatically and hissed in pain. "Oh, sorry, dear. Did that hurt?" He all but laughed at her pain, and my trigger finger twitched.

"Not as much as hearing you talk," she said, and his guys started laughing. "More than a tickle and less than paying taxes," Jen added, and the laughter continued.

"You definitely have your father's spirit, young lady," Crack said to her before pushing the blade up against her neck, right against her carotid artery. "That tongue of yours will get you in a lot of trouble. How about I carve up that pretty face of yours? After all, that face is all you have left of your whore of a mother," he added, and Jen projectiled spit at his face, streaks of blood mixed with it.

"Oh, sorry, dear. Did that hurt?" Jen mocked him, and one of his men snickered under his breath. "I think I'm keeping your boys thoroughly entertained. They might just like me more than you. At least, I'm not a backstabbing, self-centered fag," she threw at him, and he scowled. "You want me to talk? Then listen. My father talked a lot, especially when he was drunk. He would say there was only one thing worse than you, an asshole with no business in a leadership role in the club, and that was a fucking rat. I'm no rat, and I will never say who helped me get out of Sydney undetected. You can beat me until I am nothing but a head on a stick, and I will never tell you a goddamn thing." Then, she grinned triumphantly, though she still seemed weak.

"You do have a strong resolve, Jen." Crack squatted down in front of her as her eyes started to get heavy. "I've done so much to break you. I had my guys take their time with turning you into their little slut." That. Fucking. Bastard. I wanted to shoot him, but I needed to get Jen out of there. She was too close to him. I couldn't risk her getting hurt worse than she already was. "I've beat you, degraded you, thrown everything in your face. Just answer one question." She didn't react at all. Her mask of strength was holding on even in her weakened state. "Was. . .it. . .his?" Those three words seemed to torment her. Her breathing became slightly more labored. Her eyes flickered to me with panic and pleading. What was the asshole talking about? Why was it freaking her out? Crack's voice remained calm. "You held yourself together so well, and then you started bleeding. Did you already know, or did that tell you?" Then her lip started trembling. "There it is!" Then, a massive sob left her lip as her body shook. "Nothing I did broke you but losing that bastard did. No need for tears, Jennifer. It will never grow to find out how much of a whore you are." Jen couldn't even look at me, then it clicked.

Her starting to bleed, him asking who's it was, and then 'losing that bastard'. Fuck, Jen was pregnant. My girlfriend was fucking pregnant. The blood between her legs wasn't from them raping her. It was from her miscarrying.

"Xan, I'm sorry. I'm so sorry," she cried, and I frowned.

"Jen, look at me," I begged, and her eyes met mine, so full of tears and emotional torment. "You did nothing wrong, okay? None of this is your fault. We are going to get you out of here, okay?" She let out another sob, and Crack grabbed her by her hair, yanking her head back.

"You aren't going anywhere, you little slut. You are staying here, and you are going to die. Do you have any last words, Jennifer?" She started hyperventilating, then a sob broke through.

"Xander, I love you!" Oh, my god. My heart shattered a bit right there. My time had run out. I had no choice at all. I had to kill him right then and there.

I pulled the trigger, and the bullet sliced through the air, piercing his skull at his temple. Blood splattered out of the wound and stained the wall behind Jen, who gasped.

Less than a second later, everyone was opening fire. Bullets were flying through the warehouse as everyone ducked for cover. Yelps of pain and fear filled the air as everyone ran for cover.

I ducked down and jumped behind wooden crates, slowly making my way to my girl.

"Jen?!" I yelled for her and peeked around a corner. Her chair had flipped on its side, and she was fighting the restraints.

"Xander!" she called out, and I sighed.

"I'm coming for you! Just hold on!" Then, I saw a guy from their side make his way over to her and work at the rope of her restraints.

What the fuck? Wasn't he on their side? I took my chances and ran straight for Jen.

"Xander!" she cried for me, as I got to her and the guy was working at the rope around her feet.

"I'm here, baby." I looked to the guy working on freeing her legs as I stroked her hair. "Who the fuck are you?"

"A friend of Jen's. I signed up for this trip to protect her, but I failed. Why the fuck didn't you get out of the house when I told you to?" he asked her as he got her legs freed, and she started coughing.

"I'm a stubborn motherfucker, James." James? As in the guy she gave her virginity to, James?

"James Schmidt?" I asked, and he grinned. He helped me get Jen to her feet, and we dragged her toward the door. James had his gun drawn and was returning fire to his own people.

"Traitor!" someone called, and we ducked behind a crate to dodge a bullet from some bodybuilder from their side.

"I see you've been talking about me, huh?" James said to her, and she coughed out a chortle.

"Only bad things, I swear, and it was Meg." He nodded. If it wasn't for her saying it sucked really bad when they fucked, I might be jealous of him helping, but Jen needed a doctor. She was badly hurt.

"Do you have a doc on your payroll?" James asked.

"Yeah. He's fifteen minutes away." We ran with her to the door and managed to get out unscathed. James led us to the black van from outside Liam's house earlier. James threw open the side door, and I gasped from seeing Domino lying bloodied on the floor.

Domino was supposed to be on vacation with his family. How the hell did they have him?

"What the fuck happened?" I asked as James and I got Jen in the back.

"He tried to stop them before they got to the house. He saw them with Laura outside the bar. He knew something was wrong. Domino?" Jen said then cried as I laid her down, and we both saw Domino's vacant eyes.

He was dead. Fuck. Just Fuck. He didn't deserve this.

"You stay back here with her. I'll drive." I nodded in agreement as Jen laid on the floor.

"Xander?" she whispered my name, and I stroked her swollen, pale face.

"Shh, it's okay. We're going to get you fixed up, okay? You're going to be fine," I swore, and her lip trembled as her eyes met mine. The van started and sped off.

"I love you," she declared, her voice shaking and cracking.

"I love you, too, baby. I love you so much, Jen." Then she sobbed.

"Now he tells me..." I couldn't help the chuckle that broke past my lips at her quip.

"I should've told you a long time ago." She slowly nodded.

"I didn't think I'd ever get to tell you. I thought that I was never going to see you again, but you found me." She smirked at me, and I nodded, stroking her face.

"I'd never stop looking for you. You're everything to me. You can thank Drill for that later though."

"Drill? Wasn't he discharged?"

"It's a long story, but he saw them take you there and told me. Without him, I might've been too late." Her lip trembled as tears leaked from her eyes.

"I'm so sorry. I had no idea that I was pregnant. I wasn't hiding it," she cried, and I kissed her forehead softly.

"I know, babe. You did nothing wrong here. How could you have known? You had no symptoms. It's not a big deal." She shook her head vigorously.

"No, it is a big deal because I wanted it. I wanted to have that baby, and Crack took that from me. I know you said you didn't want kids, but I do. I wanted to have that baby." I took her in my arms and held her close as she cried. Yeah, if this whole thing hadn't happened, we would've had to have a massive discussion, but I wouldn't have made her have an abortion. That would've been something for us to discuss together. That wasn't the issue now. Our issue was how hurt she was by her miscarriage, and Crack used that as ammunition. He was a manipulative bastard. Thank God he's gone.

"I'm sorry I..." Jen trailed off, and I lightly shook her, but she was suddenly limping my arms. I laid her down, and her eyes were closed. Her chest didn't seem to be moving.

"Jen," I groaned her name and lightly shook her arm. "Jen!" I shook her harder and nothing else happened. Then my worst possible fear came to the forefront of my mind, nearly crippling me. "JEN! COME BACK TO ME! JEN!"

Jen wouldn't wake up.

Chapter 15

Xander

James and I rushed Jen to Dr. Hanson's house. He immediately assessed her. I was able to breathe again when he announced that she was still alive.

Jen had internal bleeding which required surgery and meant a real hospital. Things were getting complicated and fast. Jen's condition was risking putting the entire club in jeopardy. If I took her to the hospital, cops would ask questions, but I couldn't lose her.

We raced her to the hospital, and I carried her inside, wrapped in a blanket for the sake of modesty. She was taken back immediately. I wanted to go with her but the nurses, doctors, and the security guard refused to let me pass.

The waiting room set me on edge. I felt like I was stuck in an episode of Grey's Anatomy, a family member waiting for news for endless hours. Nothing felt right. Jen shouldn't be here.

Whatever doctor was working on her called the cops, and they talked to me and James separately. We already had our story down. Jen stumbled into the clubhouse how she was, and we didn't know what happened. That's what we were saying anyways. The cops didn't believe us at all. They put on a tough act, saying they would get me and my club for this. They had already decided that I'm the one who hurt Jen. It was about as much as I expected. The cops weren't helpful to people like me and my guys. Explained why we took justice into our own hands.

A couple of hours passed, and everyone from the club came to the hospital. I received the news that we had one casualty of the shoot-out. Dread, one of our newest patched members, had died, and we all grieved him and Domino as we waited for news on Jen.

As far as I could tell, Carrie and I were the only two grieving Laura.

My gut was in knots. I needed to know she was okay, and the waiting game was killing me.

Meg came and sat next to me, holding my hand tight and leaning her head on my shoulder. We waited together and silently prayed that she would be okay.

I couldn't lose Jen. She was my life, my world. I hadn't even realized how much she mattered until she was snatched. I was at the point of bargaining. I would do anything if she could be okay. I'd give up my club, get a normal job, and be with her every night. Just let her live. I was barely holding my shit together when Bruce, Sally, Liam, and Austin walked in and straight over to me. My eyes had spent so much time staring at my bloody hands that everything else seemed to have a red tint to it like a bloody photo filter.

"Where is she?" Liam asked, and my palms started to tremble.

"She's still in surgery, I think. No one has updated us," I stated with my broken voice. I was hanging on by a thread. Anything could make my resolve snap.

"What the fuck happened? You were supposed to protect her!" Liam exploded at me, and the thread snapped.

"Yeah, I was. It was my job to protect her, but every possible thing you could throw at me for this, I have already done myself. This is my fault." Tears filled my eyes as Meg rubbed my arm reassuringly.

"No, this isn't your fault, Xander. You did nothing wrong." Meg was trying her best to soothe me, but my head ended up in my hands as I cried. "Hey, she's going to be fine, okay? You did everything you were supposed to," Meg whispered to me, then I felt her kiss the back of my head. "Back off, Liam! We did everything we could." My head swirled with Jen's images and worries of never seeing her smile or laugh or just be herself. I was haunted by the picture of her in that chair in the warehouse, bloodied and battered.

"Xander?" I heard Sally's soft, sweet voice, and I slowly lifted my head. She knelt in front of me, her amber spirals surrounding her beautiful face. Her blue eyes were so sad and understanding. She stroked my face, as she frowned.

"Jen loves you, Xander," Sally muttered, softly, and my lip trembled. "I know she wouldn't blame you for this, and that is what matters. You saved her. Remember that." Then, I cried like a goddamn baby. The floodgates were slammed open, and the tears poured as my body shook.

No one who saw me then would've thought for a second that they were looking at the president of an outlaw biker gang. I had killed people, stolen, drugged up, drunk insane amounts of alcohol, and fucked my way up the west coast. I had put plenty of good men in a fucking coma, but I couldn't handle the thought of Jennifer Saunders dying. That was what broke me. Nothing else.

Sally sat in my lap and wrapped me in her arms, crying into her neck.

Sally and I weren't close by any means. We barely spoke, but she was there. That was just the kind of person she was. She started the domino effect.

136

Alexa came over and sat on the side of me opposite of Meg, and Ginger stood behind me rubbing my back soothingly. Everyone slowly surrounded me, blocking out all light that didn't come from above. They were like a security blanket, helping me grieve the inevitable.

The longer it took for us to get some news, the worse off Jen's chances were.

I clung tight to Sally as I cried and cried and cried.

I wasn't a crier. I didn't even cry when my mom or my dad died. But this was worse. This was Jen.

"Alexander Davenport?" I heard my name being called, and everyone spread out. A doctor was holding a clipboard. "I'm looking for an Alexander Davenport?" I jumped up and wiped off my face.

"That's me," my voice cracked, and he nodded.

"Come with me. We've got your wife settled." Wait, wife? I never said Jen and I were married. Why would he think that?

"So, she's okay?" The doctor nodded, as he escorted me down a long hall.

"She'll be fine. She's just a bit drained from the blood loss. She's had a transfusion which should help her replenish what she lost. We're going to keep her for a few days to be safe, but she should be in the clear. Here we are." He pointed to a door, and I rushed to it, pushing it open.

"Jen?" She was lying down in the hospital bed, partly inclined, and smirked at me as I walked in.

"Hey, you." I went straight to her and kissed her. "Mmmm," she mumbled, and I heard the doctor knock on the door.

"Don't excite yourself too much, Miss Saunders. You don't want to exacerbate your stitches." He gave a slight warning, and she nodded.

"Thanks, doc." He closed the door, and she sighed.

"How do you feel?" I asked her, and she smirked at me.

"Like I got run over by a cement truck. They've got me on a nice cocktail of drugs, but I still feel swollen everywhere," she stated weakly, and I sat beside her, careful not to hurt her, and took her hand in mine. She smirked at me.

"I'm so sorry, Jen." Then she frowned.

"Why? You didn't do anything wrong," she protested.

"I was supposed to protect you, and they snatched you when I was in the next room." She shrugged, her eyes looking heavy.

"I had a chance to escape, and I didn't. James warned me that Crack was there. He told me to slip out and get away from there," she admitted, and I went into shock for a second.

"What? Why the hell didn't you leave?" I pressed, and she smirked at me.

"I heard the others say they were going to check upstairs. They would've killed you and Meg. Your gun was downstairs. I tried to get it, but they heard me and grabbed me before I could get it. They were going to kill me right there, but James convinced them to get me out of there. He bought me some time," she explained, and I frowned.

"Shit. I hate that this happened to you." She slowly reached her hand up and touched my cheek, lightly stroking my jaw.

"You found me, Xander, and you saved me. I should be dead right now, and I'm not, thanks to you. I'm not in danger anymore because my devious uncle is dead, and I can finally stop worrying about him finding me." Jen had been worried? Fuck, how did I not know that? I'm the shittiest boyfriend ever.

"But what happened to you—"

"It's not important, Xan. I'm fine."

"Jen, he had those guys rape you. You can't say that isn't messing with you." I knew better. I remembered when it came out that some of my guys were doing that to the club girls. I remembered how Laura broke down and seemed so fragile. It was almost like she couldn't breathe thinking about it. I had witnessed that happen to my own mother. I knew better than to think Jen was okay with it.

"I saw it coming. I knew what to do to keep myself alive as long as possible. Crack wasn't even there for it. It wasn't about causing physical pain. He wanted to torture me mentally. Those guys, I knew all of them except maybe one. I'd known them my whole life. Some of them were my dad's friends as kids. I was around them a lot as a kid, and some of them didn't want to be a part of it, but they were under Crank's orders.

"Growing up, I spent a lot of time with the bikers, but I spent just as much time with the club girls. You know just as well as I do what that's like." I wanted to cry for her. "The girls at my dad's club had a trade secret of how to deal with those situations which I used. You get hurt less if you pretend you like it. If you don't fight or scream for help, they're less likely to hurt you. I was restrained anyway. I couldn't escape if I tried.

"I knew what Crack wanted. He wanted to hurt me, and I deprived him of that. He didn't want them to cause me physical pain but screw with my head by doing that and making me feel good when I didn't want it. It was about power. Crack didn't touch me, and he wasn't there, but everyone other than James participated. I know it's upsetting, but I did what I had to do." She frowned, as I squeezed her hand. Did she think I was going to be mad at her?

"I'm not upset with you, Jen. I'm pissed at them for thinking that was okay." She smirked at me.

"I'm fine, Xan. I'm just exhausted from everything," she explained, and I slowly nodded.

"Jen?" She hummed in response. "I'm sorry you lost the baby," I stated, and her eyes widened. "You know my stance on that, but I also know that was something you wanted, and I'm here if you want to talk about it." She frowned and nodded.

"I don't want to talk about it. I'd rather stuff it down and ignore it. Us being together is more important to me than my desire to procreate, so you don't need to worry." I wasn't so sure about that, but I didn't push it.

I laid down beside her, and she turned into me, pressing her face against my chest.

"I love you, Jen." She smirked before lifting her eyes toward me.

"I know. I love you, too, Xan."

Chapter 16

Xander

J en didn't say it, but I could see she was struggling. I didn't know if it was her miscarriage or her rape that was messing with her, but her spirit seemed... broken. She barely smiled, and she stopped joking around. I stopped seeing her unless I went to Liam's house.

I wanted to help her, but I just didn't know what to do. Months had passed, and she was pulling away. I could feel it. We hadn't had sex since that night, and I was fine with that. I was not going to push it. I knew she needed time to heal, even if she didn't realize it. When she was ready, I knew she would let me know.

I needed some advice, bad. I needed to know how to help her, so I went to the only two people I felt like I could. Travis 'Trip' Murphy and his wife, Danica Murphy. Travis was my VP, and Danica was the only woman he had ever loved. He'd been in love with her since they were kids.

Danica had just given birth to their daughter, Azalea, so I had given Travis some time to be at home with his family.

I drove up to their house and gently knocked on the front door. It took a few minutes, but the door opened, and Danica's mom, Denise Malenkov greeted me. Word was that she and Danica's dad got divorced a while back, so she went back to her maiden name. She was a sweetheart, much like Danica.

"Xander!" She hugged me. I knew she was a bit sweet on me, but I didn't mind.

"Hey, Denise. How's Azalea?" She grinned big as she led me inside.

"She's an angel. Are you here to see Travis?" she asked. Denise was completely clueless about the club. She didn't even know Travis wasn't some biker bar owner. They were able to hide his true occupation very well.

"Yeah, how are they?"

"Great. Dani is really drained. I'm here to help with the baby, but you know my daughter. She's as stubborn as a mule. She wants to spend all of her time with her daughter instead of resting." I nodded, as Danica and Travis walked in. Danica was glowing, holding her tiny bundle in her arms. She looked so fucking happy.

For a fraction of a second, while looking at Danica, I saw Jen standing there holding a baby in her arms looking so deliriously happy. Fuck. That was going to keep screwing with my head.

Jen had been pregnant with my kid. Just Fuck. Shit-fuck. She lost the kid, and she fucking wanted to have my kid. I still couldn't wrap my head around that. Why the fuck would Jen want to have a kid with an old fucker like me? I'm forty-six for fuck's sake. Sure, Jen was only twenty-eight, but she shouldn't want to have a kid with me.

Yet she did. Did she just love me that much?

"Xander, hey!" Danica walked over and gave me a one-armed hug. I could see Travis seemed a bit uneasy, and I frowned. Ever since he found out that

Danica and I fucked one time over a decade ago, he's had an issue with us being close, like he thought I might try to steal her. I wouldn't do that shit to him, and I doubted Danica would let me even if I wanted to. I didn't though. Danica wasn't my type which sounds strange when you think about it.

"Hey, guys. Have you been recovering okay?" I asked Danica, as she pulled away, and she nodded.

"She's pretty needy, but she's such a sweetheart. I wouldn't trade her for anything in the world. You never really know how you'll feel about having such a tiny bundle depending on you until it happens. I just can't put her down." Her statement lodged a block in my throat, making my heart race. Was that how it would be if Jen ended up pregnant again? Would my issues not even matter? "How's Jen?" Danica asked, and I frowned.

"I actually wanted to talk to you guys about that." Danica and Travis looked to Denise. It was a simple signal. 'This is a private issue.' It was simple, and she got it.

"I'll take Azalea so you can relax. We'll just be in the next room," Denise offered, and Danica hesitated.

"Darling, it's okay." Travis stroked her back affectionately, and she conceded. She eased her daughter into her mother's arms. Denise disappeared into the living room, and the three of us took a seat at the table. I watched as Danica slipped into Travis's lap, and his arms wrapped around her waist.

I had to sigh. That used to be me and Jen until her twisted uncle abducted her.

"She hasn't gotten any better?" Danica asked, and I shrugged.

"No, she hasn't. She's been drawing into herself, and she barely talks. I don't know what to do." Travis nodded with a frown on his face.

"Damn," he muttered.

"Xander, you don't get it. It's hard when you've been through what she went through. It's hard to deal with and even harder to talk about it. You end up thinking it was something you did or said that caused it, especially if you don't open up about it. You can feel guilty and, if Jen feels that way, she would be understandably pulling away from you. The guilt, if you're in a relationship, can make you feel in a sense like you cheated on that person." That made a lot of sense. She did expect me to be upset with her that day in the hospital.

"I don't know what to do to help her," I said defeated, and Danica placed her hand on top of mine, understanding radiating from her.

"Xander, you can't help her. She has to help herself. The only thing you can do to ease her mind is to make sure she knows that it doesn't matter what happened to her. You still love her, and you don't think any less of her. She's still the same woman, and she needs to see that you believe that." I was grateful for that advice.

"But I'm not so sure it's what those guys did to her that's making her pull away." Danica looked at me confused. It was then that I knew that Travis never told Danica what everyone in the club had found out that night. She had to stay behind because we didn't want to risk her getting hurt with her being pregnant. "Jen was pregnant," I admitted, and Danica gasped.

"You-you mean when she-she was taken?" I slowly nodded.

"They beat her until it died. Crack used that to break her mentally." Danica's eyes started to tear up, probably imagining how she would've felt if she lost Azalea when she was pregnant.

"Oh, my god." Danica slowly shook her head before speaking again. "All you can do is be there for her and listen to whatever she wants to talk about concerning it. You can't take away her pain. You can help ease it when it gets unbearable. She needs a partner, not someone telling her how she should feel or act. She needs support that only you can provide."

Chapter 17

Jen

I laid in my bed, relaxing. I was trying to ignore the string of texts from James. He and the other Black Stallions in Sydney were begging me to come back, but I just couldn't even think about it. A visit even seemed like too much. The thought made me feel like I was suffocating. All I could see when I thought of home was Crack and his evil smile. I knew he was dead, but I couldn't get away from him.

It was almost like that was his mission. He was haunting me and left me in a crippled state. I could hardly handle being near Xander, and it had nothing to do with me or him. I felt bad because I knew Xander thought he was doing something wrong even if he tried to hide it.

Maybe he would be better off without me. Had I become an unnecessary stressor for him? I frowned from the thought.

Suddenly, there was a knock at my bedroom door, and I slowly sat up.

"Yeah?" I spoke softly.

"It's me, babe. Can I come in?" It was Xander. I was anxious. I didn't want to see that pity on his face, but I also missed him when he was gone.

146

"Yeah, come in." The door opened, and Xander strolled in holding a bouquet of snow bells, a smirk across his face. Xander walked over and took a seat next to me.

"Hey, beautiful." He leaned over and gave me the sweetest, gentlest kiss on the lips before sensually laying the flowers in my lap.

"Snow bells? What's the occasion?" I asked, surprised. He tucked a stray hair behind my ear.

"No occasion, babe. I just know they're your favorite." And like that, I was smiling.

That was Alexander Davenport for you. The simplest action from him could put a smile on my face and erase all the sadness and anxiety I felt.

"Thanks. They're beautiful." He could be so fucking sweet.

He kissed me again and pressed his forehead against me.

"I love you, Jen." It had been so long since he had said those words to me. I was starting to wonder if he still felt that way about me. They filled me with love and euphoria.

"I love you, too," I whispered and wrapped my arms around him. He took me in his arms, and my whole body relaxed.

"Jen?" I looked into his eyes and sighed. I saw it there. The worry. I hated it, yet I knew it was warranted. "I know you're dealing with a lot of stuff. I know it's going to take a while to work through it all, and I'm here whenever you need me, okay? You're still my Jen, and I love you so fucking much." God. So sweet.

I pressed my mouth against his, and it felt like all tension left me.

"Thank you," I whispered, as I ran my fingers through his hair, loving the softness against my fingers. "I think I'd like to go outside." He grinned big.

"That sounds like a great idea, babe."

"Can we go for a ride on your bike?" I asked, and his grin got even bigger.

"Most definitely, babe."

* * *

It was good to get out of the house. Maybe my problem was being alone all the time. Xander was so damn supportive. It made my heart melt.

A few days after our ride, Xander picked me up for us to have a date. It wasn't one of our normal dates. We used to get takeout and sit on the picnic table outside his cabin. This was us both dressed up in a real restaurant.

I knew most girls wanted their man to take them to high-end restaurants, but I didn't need that, and it wasn't Xander's comfort zone.

I was beyond shocked when Xander's pickup truck pulled up in front of Le Papillon.

The parking lot was full of expensive cars and the building was surrounded by flower bushes of a rainbow of colors and there was a stone path that led from the sidewalk to the front door.

I looked at him surprised, and he smirked as he climbed out. I followed after him, and he took my hand, smiling happily at me.

"Okay, you've officially made me suspicious." He laughed and threw his arm around my shoulder. "What's the occasion?"

"The occasion is I love you, and I want to show off my gorgeous girlfriend." He winked at me and escorted me inside.

This place was reservation-only. Alexander Davenport actually had a reservation for us? What the heck was going on?

Holy. Shit. Was he planning to... propose? Was that why we were having an expensive date? My heart started racing.

The hostess escorted us to a table where me and Xander sat close together, his arm around my shoulder.

"You look amazing, Jen." God, please, lay on the flattery.

"You look pretty good yourself." He did, too. He had a nice button-down over his dark jeans and his arms were bulging through the shirt. It was a shame that none of his tattoos were visible. I loved Xander's tattoos.

He bent his head down and kissed me passionately. I got lost in the feeling and forgot for a moment that we were in public. I slipped my hand up his leg, and he groaned. My finger hit the tip of his hard dick in his pants, and my clit buzzed. Fuck. It had been so long since Xander and I had sex or even any type of sexual touching.

I fucking wanted him and a big part of me wanted to drop to my knees right there and take his massive cock in my mouth. I was quickly getting wet, and my finger had barely grazed his sex.

149

Damn. I needed him to fuck me soon. It was a good thing we were in a secluded corner with no one else around.

"Xan," I moaned and dove my tongue past his lips. I took his hand and slid it up my thigh, past the hem of my dress, and under my thong. He groaned and kissed me harder, as he started to finger me, soft and slow. God, I forgot how good that felt.

"Fuck, baby." He released my lips and started kissing his way down my neck.

I had been worried that I might freak out on him the first time he touched me like this, but I wasn't struggling at all.

"Oh, my god. I want you, Xander." He nodded against my neck, breathing hard.

"You're so fucking wet. I missed touching you like this."

"It's been too long. I need your cock inside me," I whispered, and he growled.

"Shit, Jen. You can have it all you want once we leave here. I doubt anyone wants to see me pounding you on this table." Then, he added another finger, and I spread my legs more for him.

"Xan, please. Harder. Play with my clit, baby." He nodded and obeyed me. Yes. That was it. I loved that Xander didn't treat me like a porcelain doll. If he wanted to, he would throw me against a wall and fuck me until my body was covered in bruises and semen. He wasn't afraid to fuck me like he meant it, and I loved it.

"I'm going to fuck you so good tonight, baby. Pound your sweet pussy until you can't orgasm anymore. Would you like that? My cock inside your tightness all night long? Mmmm, so fucking good." Oh. My. God. Yes.

"Yes, yes, yes. I'm so close." I whimpered then kissed him. I couldn't take the chance that I screamed out in the middle of a restaurant when I orgasmed. I kissed him hard and clamped down on him, whining and moaning into his eager lips. I rode his hand to extend my orgasm, and the aftershock was fucking incredible.

I could breathe a sigh of relief that I hadn't freaked out on Xander. I was so worried about that. I didn't want him to think that it was him. Xander was so amazing, and it felt like I didn't need to worry about that. I was a strong woman, and I had bounced back.

"Thank you for that, babe," Xander whispered to me before licking his fingers clean. I rubbed my hand back up his leg and rubbed his full hardness. He groaned with need.

"Mmmm, you are so getting laid tonight." He laughed at that, and we ignored the cloud of lust surrounding us.

* * *

The food was excellent, and I enjoyed having a real date with Xander. It was nice to sit together in a public setting and just talk. I had missed this, just being with him. For the longest time, it felt like he had to tip-toe his way around me and be careful about what he said, but it was different now. I had done a lot of healing in the past couple of days, and I finally felt like I was ready to get back to how we used to be. He seemed prepared for it, too. We had talked a lot about what happened to me and losing the baby. We never addressed his feelings about being a father. I knew that would probably never change, but he was there for me and supportive of my desires to be a mother. He even said that he would understand if at some point we broke up just because of me wanting to be a mother. I shut him down right there. If us being together meant I never got to have children, I would deal with it. Nothing had ever felt as right as being with Xander.

Xander and I walked back to his truck. I pulled him against me and molested his tasty mouth. He groaned and held my body tight against his.

"God, Jen. Are you sure you're ready for this?" I nodded, eagerly.

"Yeah, I want you. Can we go to your place? It would probably be best not to fuck at Liam's house. I swear, I need my own place. He puts his nose in my business too much." He gave me a big grin at that.

"Let's go, babe." We hopped into his truck, and he turned in the opposite direction out of the parking lot than I expected. What the hell?

"I thought we were going to your house?" He slowly nodded.

"We are." No, we weren't. We were going the wrong way! What was he up to?

"Then, why are we going this way?"

"You'll see." Xander drove a couple of miles before he turned into a suburban neighborhood full of decent houses. They were nice.

He turned down a street and pulled up to a house at the end of the cul-de-sac. It had gray siding, red bricks, black shutters, and a mahogany front door. Gray stones created a path from the sidewalk to the white, wooden porch complete with a porch swing connected to the roof by silver chains. The path was lined with white daffodils and marigolds and vines of red roses lined the porch perfectly.

It was beautiful. It reminded me of the pictures my mom showed me when I was a little girl of her childhood home. It exuded... normalcy and peace.

"What are we doing here?" I asked, as we got out of the truck. He came straight to me and took me in his arms.

"This is the house I bought for us." Wait, what? Us? Holy crap. Was he asking me to move in with him? Tonight wasn't about a proposal. Xander was just leading up to showing me the house.

"Us?" I asked, surprised, and he smirked.

"Well, you did say you needed to move out of Liam's house." I hurriedly kissed him with everything I had in me, clinging to him. I was so happy that I could cry but I wouldn't.

"Are you sure?" I asked him, and he grinned.

"Most definitely, babe. There is only one downside to this place, a single annoyance that resides two doors down." He explained and, for some reason, I thought he was going to tell me Keyanna, his ex, lived there with her husband and kid. That would be a huge problem. Keyanna has a huge issue with me. Probably because I didn't put up with her shit or her disrespecting my man. It was possible because I punched her when she made a snide remark about my man being a thug. She wasn't even strong enough to try to hit me back. The girl just ran off. Probably the only reason I didn't go to jail was because she had already given birth. "Damn Sage Smith is a pain in my ass." I was a bit surprised by that.

"Um, who?" He let out a masculine chortle before kissing my forehead.

"Sally's little sister. She's like that annoying little sister you just can't shake." Suddenly, his face fell like he had an unpleasant thought.

"Xan, what's wrong?" I was concerned. He rarely ever had that look. It was usually bad news when he did.

"Nothing," he tried to deflect, but I wasn't fooled.

"Tell me," I demanded, as I took his hands in mine, offering my support for whatever it was.

"It's just my sister's birthday is all." Shock and disbelief surfaced in me from the words he spoke.

"Sister? You have a sister?" He nodded and laughed from the look on my face.

"Is that so surprising?"

"Yes! I mean, no. I mean, you've never mentioned your sister. Why have I never met her?" I was completely taken by surprise by this.

"Probably because I haven't even seen her since the day she was born twenty years ago." Oh god.

"What happened?" I asked.

"My dad made my mom give her away." What. The. Fuck. "He was the president, and his word was law. Austin and I were never given a reason. We didn't get it at all. That was the first time I challenged my father and how I ended up with this." He pointed to the scar on his eye. Holy shit. "I was pissed. My mom was a mess, and my dad was a jackass. He didn't care how anyone else felt about it. For some reason, he did not want her." Xander said all of it with a straight face like he had said it a million times before.

"Xander, that's horrible." I just wanted to hold him.

"Austin and I tried looking for her with no luck."

"What was her name?" I asked, and he smirked.

"Cheyenne," he stated, and I frowned. Cheyenne. Such a nice name. I bet she was pretty. I had seen pictures of Xander's parents. His father had dark brown, nearly black hair, and he had Xander's eyes. His mother was gorgeous. Light, honey blonde hair, lilac eyes, plump lips, and high cheekbones. She had a special look compared to normal club girls. She had that nice college girl look about her.

I was shocked to find out that Xander's mom was the same woman who had the mural on the Black Stallions bar's side. That gorgeous woman I had admired the first day I met Xander.

Crank had told me that Davina Deveraux, Xander's mom, had a sad story. She was a sweet girl in college and started dating a guy named Galen Mayes. A month into dating, he joined the Black Stallions. Since he was a prospect, everything that was his became the club's property, even the girl he barely started dating.

Davina was tossed around a lot, raped repeatedly, and got pregnant by the president from being broken in. She was a favorite of his, and his Sergeant In Arms. There had been rules set in place that she was a piece of property that could only be touched by the top five. She was their 'diamond piece'. She was a trophy fuck to them.

Davina got pregnant with Xander, and she was suddenly treated with the highest respect just because the president raped her and his child was more valuable than anyone else's. Most presidents would have claimed her just for that, but he didn't. He let his friends continue to use her. He didn't care.

She was even beaten into an early labor for no reason whatsoever.

Crank tried to protect her, but there was only so much he could do.

I never got to meet her, but I had a large amount of respect for Davina Deveraux. She went through so much that she didn't ask for and still she raised the most amazing man, the man I loved, Xander.

Out of nowhere, Xander's phone started to ring. I pulled away from him as he pulled it out and my eyes scanned the beautiful front yard.

"Hey. . .what?" His voice was sharp, and I turned my head to see shock across his face. He stumbled back a bit and leaned against his truck, disbelief across his face. "Really? Yeah, thanks." Then, he hung up and looked at me with eyes so full of emotion, I wouldn't have been surprised if he started crying.

"What's wrong?" I asked.

"Laura." I wasn't sure who had done it but someone called for an ambulance for Laura once everything was over in the warehouse. She was rushed to the hospital, barely hanging on, and had been in a coma ever since.

"What about her?" I asked, and he smirked.

"She's awake."

Epilogue

Liam

I hated, absolutely fucking hated Gunner a.k.a. Xander. I always had. He was such a cocky asshole but now my hatred was at its max. The bastard had his eye on my cousin, Jen, of all people. Jen wasn't sweet and innocent but she had been through enough fucking shit without Xander setting his sights on her.

The asshole had every biker girl at his disposal but no that wasn't good enough for him. No, he had to have Jen. It pissed me off.

I saw him sitting on one of the loungers with his phone out. He had that disgusting flirtatious smirk on his face. I didn't need to see what he was texting or reading. I knew it was about my cousin.

I was pissed.

I strolled right over to him and he looked up at me expectantly with a bit of annoyance.

"What's up, Liam?" he muttered and I scowled at him.

"I'm not kidding. Stay the hell away from Jen, period. If you even look in her general direction, I'll kill you myself." That was all I said, and I walked off.

I was so livid that I almost didn't notice Laura, one of the biker girls, climbing out of the pool.

Goddamnit. Laura was stunning as always. She was wearing a black tankini with big red polka dots. Water was draining down her body from her gorgeous light blonde hair and it flowed down her sun-kissed skin. That woman had the body of a swimsuit model with bigger tits. Instead of the perky kiwis that women her size tended to have, Laura was blessed with a pair of California oranges. They were even perky at that size. They looked so scrumptious. Her legs went on for days and her ass had a string of fantasies dedicated to it.

"Hey, Liam," Laura uttered as she was ringing out her hair, sending me a flirtatious smirk. God, what I would give to have those cotton candy pink lips of hers wrapped around my cock.

Yes, I fucking lusted after Laura. I had wanted to fuck that woman for years and I knew she did, too. I caught her staring at me multiple times over the years, usually when my t-shirt was a bit snug or my jeans hung a bit low on my waist. Laura and I flirted a bit but nothing ever happened. It wasn't that we didn't want it to.

We knew the rules. The biker girls weren't allowed to fuck or date anyone outside of the club. They were "mouses" which meant they had no say in who they screwed. I didn't know exactly what would happen if we did but I didn't want to find out. My life wasn't worth the forbidden fruit. It might last an hour if I was lucky, but then it would be over and all of the bikers who protected me and the band would be gunning for me.

Laura was smoking hot, but it wasn't worth it.

"Hey, Laura," I greeted her back and winked flirtatiously at her. I caught her biting her lip at me as I kept walking off.

Laura was so distracting that I completely forgot what had me so pissed off a minute ago. I couldn't recall it but it didn't matter right then. I needed to escape so I could beat my meat to avoid doing something fucking stupid.

Like fucking Laura Murdoch.

About the Author

Ava West is a romance author who dabbles on the less fluffy side of fiction. Her books contain dark themes with happy endings. She lives in Texas with her husband, three children, and enjoys spending her downtime binge watching The Vampire Diaries.

You can connect with me on:

🌐 https://avawestauthor.wixsite.com/website

📘 https://www.facebook.com/Ava-West-Romance-Author-104796658244448

CPSIA information can be obtained
at www.ICGtesting.com
Printed in the USA
BVHW071035050521
606424BV00008B/1318